CW01432884

T. Csernis & Julia Bland

FORBIDDEN BOND
A NUMENVERSE COMPANION STORY

NUMENVERSE

Copyright © 2024 by Tate Csernis (T. Csernis).

All rights reserved. No part of this book may be used or reproduced in any form whatsoever without written permission except in the case of brief quotations in critical articles or reviews.

Without limiting the author's exclusive rights, any unauthorised use of this publication to train generative artificial intelligence (AI) technologies is expressly prohibited.

This book is a work of fiction. Names, characters, businesses, organizations, places, events, and incidents either are the product of the author's imagination or are used fictitiously. Any resemblance to actual persons, living or dead, events, or locales is entirely coincidental.

For more information on the world, this series, other books, or to contact the author, head to: https://www.numenverse.com/

Cover created by Julia Bland

ISBN – Paperback: 978-1-917270-01-4
ISBN – Hardcover: 978-1-917270-02-1
ISBN – E-Book: 978-1-917270-03-8

THE NUMEN CHRONICLES is a collaborative work written by

Tate Csernis (T. Csernis) and Julia Bland (Julia B.)

Each Party retains ownership over their respected Intellectual Property created outside of this collaboration, including but not limited to names, characters, stories, etc. All Collaborative Intellectual Property shall be jointly owned by the Parties, and each Party shall have the right freely to use all Collaborative Intellectual Property for all purposes and uses.

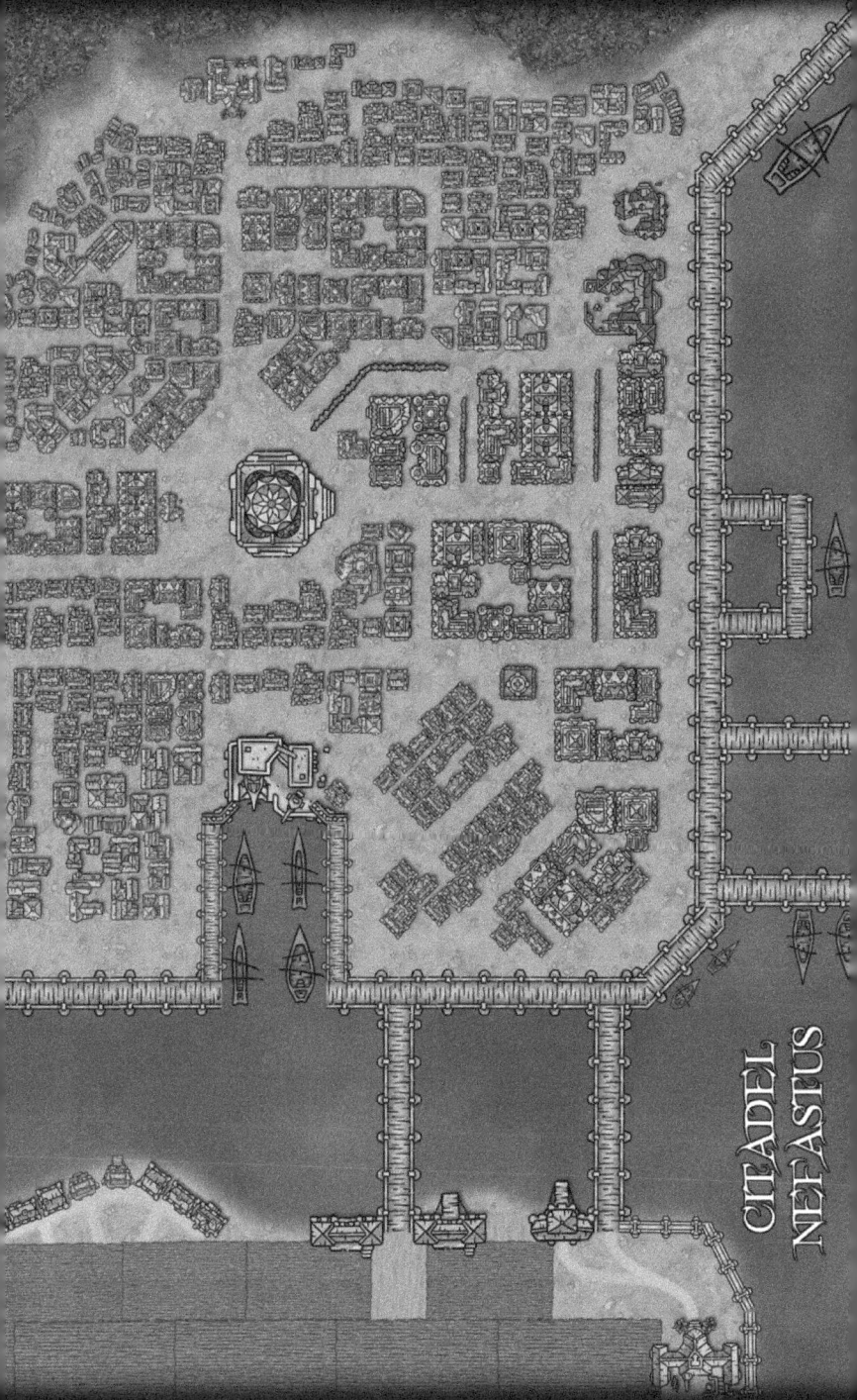

CITADEL NEFASTUS

GLOSSARY

Ethos [ee-thos] - The energy within someone that can be used to create or manipulate other energies

✝

Dor-Sanguis [door-san-goo-wis] - Translates roughly to Pain *[Portuguese]* and blood *[Latin]* (aka, Romania)

✝

Nefastus [neh-fas-tus] – Translates to Unlawful *[Latin]* (aka, the Americas)

✝

Eltaria [el-tar-ia] – Zalith's homeworld

✝

Numen [noo-men] - God-like beings that chose to show themselves to the world rather than remain anonymous

✝

Aegis [ee-gis] - The Dragon Gods, children of Letholdus

✝

DeiganLupus [day-gan-loo-pus] - Translates roughly to 'refused to turn to the wolf' *[Icelantic, Latin]* (aka, UK)

✝

Lumendatt [loo-men-dat] – Numen crystals containing the power to create life

✝

Obcasus [ob-cass-us] – Knives capable of putting Numen in a frozen statis

✝

Proselytus [pros-elly-tus] – A heart-like organ which creates ethos inside a body

✝

Scion [skee-on] – ethos-crafted children of the Numen

✝

Infățișare [in-fuh-tsee-SHAH-reh] – vampires able to shift into animal forms

✝

The Seven Realms:

Aegisguard [ee-gis-guard] - The world
(aka, Earth)
Mareaeternum [Mar-ay-ter-num] Translates to eternal tide *[Latin]*
Glaciaqua [Glass-ee-aqua]
Letholdus [Lee-fold-us]
Tengetso [Ten-get-so]
Celitrianas [Sel-it-ree-a-nas]
Yilmana [Yeel-mana]

The Months and Currency

Months

January – Primis
February – Cordus
March – Tertium
April – Aprilis
May – Quintus
June – Iunius
July – Quintilis
August – Tria
September – Novem
October – Decem
November – Undecim
December – Clausula

Currency

Copper – Equivalent of $0.01
Bronze – Equivalent of $0.20
Silver – Equivalent of $2
Gold – Equivalent of $10
Coronam – Equivalent of $100
Cidaris – Equivalent of $1 million

FORBIDDEN BOND
A Numenverse Companion Story

CONTENTS

FORBIDDEN BOND
A Numenverse Companion Story

FORBIDDEN BOND
A Numenverse Companion Story

Chapter One

»— ⟩ 𝕖 ⟨ —«

Fascination

| *Friday, Clausula 30ᵗʰ, 959(TG)—Nefastus* |

It was Yule, a night meant for celebration, and yet there Danford stood, feeling like a lonely, pathetic loser. The room buzzed with laughter and music, couples enjoying the festivities together, but he was left on the sidelines. Why did he have to stand there, watching the man who was supposed to be his boyfriend flirt shamelessly with Varana? His chest tightened with the all-too-familiar sting of betrayal. He knew— he *knew* Luther was still seeing her behind his back. And as much as he tried to deny it, a painful certainty gnawed at him: Luther would never truly choose him. He was just the piece on the side. The option. The maybe. The whatever.

His heart ached with the weight of that realization, and despite how much he wanted to confront Luther, he couldn't. Luther had made it clear—they couldn't be seen together. Varana would hurt them both, and Danford couldn't risk that. But standing there, watching the man he loved give his attention to someone else, was tearing him apart. It hurt too much, the pain twisting in his chest with every stolen glance they shared. And it was just another reminder that no one would ever really want him. This happened *all* the time. Everyone he dated left him sooner or later.

Desperation clawed at him, threatening to break through the fragile composure he clung to. He couldn't take it anymore. Swallowing back the bitter lump of sadness rising in his throat, Danford abruptly turned on his heel and headed for the door, needing to escape—

"Watch it!" Freja snapped as they collided, her voice cutting through the haze of his emotions like a knife.

Danford barely registered the collision, his mind too clouded by the storm of heartbreak and anger. All he wanted was to escape—to disappear from this suffocating party, from the unbearable reminder that the love he longed for might never be his. But when the impact finally registered, and he stumbled back, hands raised in a startled reflex, his eyes widened in shock.

"Oh—oh, my God, I'm so sorry! A-are you okay?" he stammered, his voice shaky as he stared at Freja's irritated face. Panic quickly replaced his sadness as the reality of who he'd just crashed into hit him like a second blow. Freja—the Luna of his recently extended pack. His heart pounded in his chest, certain he was about to face her wrath for his carelessness.

Freja studied him for a moment, her sharp gaze making him squirm under the weight of it. But instead of the scolding he expected, she let out a sigh and shook her head. "It's fine," she muttered, her voice softened, though her frown lingered. There was something in her expression that surprised him—concern? "Where are you going looking so sad?" she asked, her tone shifting from irritation to curiosity, her frown deepening slightly.

Danford blinked, caught off guard by her unexpected question, the knot of emotions in his chest tightening as he scrambled to find an answer. "Home," he said sullenly. "O-or I mean…to the boat," he corrected. "I'm sorry I bumped into you," he said, moving to step past her.

But Freja crossed her arms and stepped aside so that he couldn't walk past. "Why? Because of him?" she asked, nodding over his shoulder.

Danford frowned and looked back there, seeing that she was referring to Luther.

"Don't waste your time," she told him. "That man's worse than Zalith used to be from what I've heard."

He looked down at the floor as his sadness started to grip him tightly. "I don't know," he said with a shrug. "He's not perfect, but…I thought we had something."

"He makes everyone think they have something special with him. I've been working with Luther for a few years now, and the amount of people I've seen him go through is astonishing, even for someone like him. Don't let him break your heart."

Her words filled his heart with more pain. He tried his best to be what Luther wanted—what he *needed*. But nothing ever seemed to be good enough for him, and it was only now that Danford was starting to wake up. Freja's revelation made him feel embarrassed because he didn't want to end up being played again; he just wanted someone to love who loved him back the same way, not someone who loved him when it suited them. Luther wasn't who he thought he was; he wasn't who Danford tried so hard to believe he was. He was using him, wasn't he? And he had been from the start.

He didn't want to stay there a moment longer. It was a party, and he didn't want to be crying—and it was also Yule, a time of year that *everyone* spent with their loved ones. He didn't have anyone, really…so maybe he would be better off alone on the ship.

"Oh," he said sadly in response to what Freja said. "I should…get going," he said, moving to walk past her again—but as she had the first time, she stopped him.

"Are you looking forward to moving off the boat?" she asked, changing the subject.

Danford stared at her for a moment. He didn't want to be rude; she was actually being a lot nicer to him than he thought she might be. He stopped trying to leave and nodded. "Yeah, it'll be nice. I'm getting tired of being on the water all the time."

She smiled. "Do you miss the forest? The grass?"

He nodded shyly as he glanced at her curious face. "Yeah, I really do. I used to love going out into the woods to find somewhere nice to sit down and draw for the day."

"Oh, I've seen you sitting around drawing from time to time, but I've never actually seen any of your stuff. Maybe you can show me sometime," she suggested, still smiling at him.

Danford felt surprised and confused; had someone sent her over to talk to him because they'd seen that he looked sad? Had Greymore sent her? What would someone like her want with someone like him?

He then realized that he was just staring at her and hadn't replied. "U-uh... yeah, sure, I can show you whenever," he agreed. "I have a lot of drawings in my room—n-not that we have to go to my room or anything," he then insisted, his heart starting to race as angst gripped him tightly. He didn't want her to get the wrong impression. "I can show you up on the deck... o-or in the bar—but you don't have to get a drink or anything, I probably won't drink, I'll just be... at the table, or something," he said so quickly that he had to take a deep breath once he was done.

But Freja giggled, holding her hand over her mouth as she did.

She probably thought he was an idiot, didn't she? He lowered his head and stared sullenly at the floor below. "Sorry," he said.

Freja frowned and stopped giggling. "Why are you sorry?"

"Because I'm embarrassing."

She laughed again but placed her hand on the side of his arm. "You're not embarrassing. You're actually the most tolerable out of everyone I've spoken to tonight," she said with a sigh.

As his eyes widened in shock, he glanced at her hand. Why was she touching him? She was so nice—but why? He was just a boring, weak nobody. He frowned and looked at her. "T-thank you. Are... are you not having a nice time?"

Taking her hand off his arm, she sipped from her drink and shrugged. "I'm having a nice time, it's just hard to find someone who isn't so loud. You'll find that a lot of the men here are not only too loud for their own good but really don't know how to hold a conversation, either."

"They're not *so* bad once you get to know them," Danford said. "But I agree... I just keep to myself mostly—n-not because I think I'm better than them, though. I'm just more introverted," he said quickly, once again having to take a breath after.

She giggled in response. "I've been here long enough to get to know what I need to know about everyone, but all I really know about you is that you're a bit of a quiet one

---

and one particularly good at drawing. If you still want to leave, I won't stop you, but I think I might actually enjoy a little more of your time."

Danford so very swiftly became enthralled with confliction. He looked back over his shoulder to where Luther had been standing, but he wasn't there anymore, and he wasn't anywhere to be seen, either. He wasn't by any of the refreshment or food tables, nor was he near the door or talking to anyone or dancing. He was gone, and Danford suspected that he must have wandered off with Varana, who was also now nowhere to be seen.

He felt as if he'd like to stay and talk to Freja; they could be friends…or something…whatever an Omega could be to a Luna. But he didn't want Luther to see them—if he came back, that was. He might get mad and jealous—but…maybe he deserved to see how it felt to deal with those feelings in *silence* whenever he saw Luther with Varana.

But then he scowled. It wasn't like anything was ever going to happen between him and Freja; she was an Alpha and better than him in so many ways. She was *far* out of his league, and the most they would probably ever be was friends. But that was okay because he actually liked the idea of that.

Sighing, he shrugged. He wanted to go back to the boat and dwell in his sadness, but…he was also having a nice time talking to her and thought that maybe it would be better to stay in the company of someone who somehow made him feel better. So, he nodded. "I'll stay," he agreed.

"Great," she said with a smile, taking his arm in hers. "Let's go over here and get a drink."

"O-oh, okay, sure," he agreed, following as she dragged him off into the crowd. Maybe he didn't have to spend all night in a pit of depression after all.

When they reached the mini bar, Freja ordered two martinis, and then she took Danford over to an empty table.

"So, why Luther?" she asked as they sat down. "What did you even see in him?"

Danford sighed deeply, staring into his drink. "I don't know. He was just…there was something about him, I guess. He was nice to me, which was a rare occurrence since a lot of the pack look at me like I'm just some…I don't know—"

"Like you're just another grunt? Just another Omega?"

He nodded. "I mean they don't hate me or anything, they just don't really put much effort into talking to or getting to know me."

"I've always found it a little sad that Omegas are treated so poorly. I mean, I've seen worse, but your situation is no less upsetting. Have you talked to Greymore about it? He's a bit much personality-wise, but he seems to care."

Danford shook his head. "Nah, I mean…*he's* okay. He's nice to me whenever he's around me. But I don't wanna make a fuss. Like I said, I'm fine with being in the background."

Freja frowned curiously. "Yeah, but if you're always so far in the back, how are you going to meet someone who actually cares about you and doesn't treat you like a cigarette?"

He lifted his head to glance unsurely at her. "A... cigarette?"

"Yeah. Gets what he needs from you and then tosses you into the grass, possibly starting a forest fire," she joked, giggling a little.

Danford smiled slightly, admittedly amused, but the sadness clung onto him like a tick, slowly feeding off any emotion other than his dismay. "I don't know, I guess I kinda just... lost hope a while ago."

Freja sipped from her drink and asked, "Lost hope in what?"

He felt nervous about answering. Was it because Freja was his superior, or was it because saying the words would make him feel like even more of a loser? He wasn't sure, but what he *was* sure of was that he didn't want to seem rude. So he fiddled with his eyepatch and quietly said with a shrug, "In finding my mate. I feel like... maybe I'm one of those wolves who'll never find them."

She scoffed and shook her head. "*Every* wolf has a mate, Danford."

"I've heard stories, though—"

"Stories?"

He nodded. "Stories of wolves who got old and died before their mate showed up."

She laughed dismissively. "Oh, those are just scary stories that parents tell their pups. You'll find them. Perhaps the Herald will help you."

Danford frowned, staring across the table at her. "Sorry, the what?"

"The Herald."

He had no idea what that was.

"Oh... maybe you had a different name for it in Eltaria. It's what we call the week before the full moon. The moon's power begins to grow stronger, and it affects us werewolves more. There are a lot of stories, of course, and I believe them all."

Intrigued, Danford rested his arms on the table.

Freja continued, "During this time, some wolves can dream and see through their ancestors' eyes; some relive significant moments in their past which have turned out to help them with something they were struggling with, such as their purpose or finding something, such as their mate. We believe that the Herald is the Moon Goddess' way of reminding us of who we are, how powerful we can really be, and where we truly belong."

Danford wasn't just captivated by her words—he found himself drawn to her in a way that went beyond mere fascination. There was something almost mesmerizing about the way she moved, a subtle grace in every gesture. As she brought her glass to her lips, the dim light of the party hall caught the shimmer of her golden eyes, making them glow softly. Her lips puckered slightly as she sipped, the motion delicate, deliberate. It was a simple action, yet Danford couldn't tear his eyes away. Every movement seemed to hold a quiet elegance that left him momentarily entranced.

"Oh, do you howl to the Moon Goddess in Eltaria?" she asked.

He snapped out of his trance. "Uh…" he drawled. "Um…no, sorry. I…I uh…" he paused and exhaled, trying to recollect himself. "We howled to the Lunar Empress."

Freja looked like she was pondering. "Hmm…I wonder if they're the same deity."

"Maybe," he mumbled. Despite the fascination drawing him towards Freja, he couldn't help but look over his shoulder and search the hall for Luther. But there was no sign of him. Had he left with Varana? Probably.

"Should we get out of here?" Freja asked.

Startled by both her question and her forwardness, Danford felt flustered, and he knew his cheeks went red, so he turned his head away. "Oh…uh…like…to a bar or something?" he asked nervously. They'd barely had one drink.… Things were moving a little fast, but he wasn't against it. He did like the idea of not being in the same place as Luther and Varana right now.

She finished her drink and rested her arms on the table, leaning forward a little. "Sure. We could head to the one on the ship."

"The ship…where I'm staying?"

Freja laughed lightly. "Yes, Danford. The bar on the ship where you're staying. Or there's a little place not far from the docks if that'd make you more comfortable; to be honest, I'm sure the ship's bar is packed with Greymore's loud packmates."

His heart beat a little faster as his nervousness intensified. But…he didn't want to say no. Something—no…*everything* inside him urged him to say yes; the feeling was almost desperate, and it shoved aside his sadness. And he let the words slip from his mouth, "Okay, sure."

She smiled excitedly, but there was also relief on her face. "Are you going to finish your martini?"

Danford glanced down at his drink. "Oh…uh.…" He didn't want to be rude, so he picked it up and downed it in a few sips. "Okay," he said, holding his hand over his mouth, trying to avoid looking sloppy and disgusting. "B-but…what about the other packs?" he remembered. "Greymore hasn't finished making agreements with them; w-what if we like…bump into one of them and they start a fight."

Freja laughed a little. "This place is well within our territory, don't worry."

He still felt a little unsure about it; the last thing he wanted was to start a turf war, but if Freja insisted it was safe, then he trusted her. "Okay," he said shyly. "We can go."

She stood up, and when Danford did, she smiled and started leading the way through the bustling party.

His heart was pounding, and his legs felt like jelly. Part of him wondered whether this was actually happening, whether the pack Luna was actually leaving the party with *him*. Was she doing it because she felt sorry for him? She obviously knew that Luther had dumped him. If that *was* the case, he didn't mind. Someone to talk to was better than sitting around alone moping.

But... why *her*? He was a loser. Why would an Alpha care? A part of him wanted to feel skeptical, especially after how Luther had been treating him, but it felt... wrong. Was it instinct? Were his instincts assuring him that he didn't have to feel cautious around Freja? Maybe... maybe not. He wasn't sure. But he wanted to go with her. So as the party continued behind him, and while Luther was wherever he was with Varana, he followed Freja out the glass doors.

A lingering thought stabbed into his heart, though. Would Luther come crawling back to him tonight... or was he going to spend another night alone?

Chapter Two

>— ☽ 🐇 ☾ —≺

Rosemary Inn

The carriage ride into the was a little awkward. Danford sat on one side, and Freja sat on the other, and neither of them said a word. Unsure whether she was waiting for *him* to start a conversation, Danford attempted to think of something to talk about, but he was so nervous and confused and upset that all he could think about was Luther. Despite knowing that man would never love him the way he wanted, he just couldn't let go.

When the carriage lightly jolted, Freja giggled and glanced out the window. "I think we hit a rock or something."

"Sorry, sir, ma'am," the coachman called from outside.

Danford chuckled nervously. "Yeah, I think we did."

A curious gaze appeared on her face while she stared out the window. "What was it like in Eltaria? The forests, the trees. Was it the same as Aegisguard?"

"Well, it smelled different over there. The earth here feels kinda different…and a little unkind somehow." He sighed deeply. "I don't know. I don't really know if this is where I should be if I'm being honest. I'd go back if I had the choice."

Freja frowned. "Back to a world ravaged by war, a place where our kind are hunted down like dogs and turned into coats and rugs?"

"It never used to be like that."

"What did it use to be like?"

"Peaceful," he answered, reminiscing. "I mean not for everyone all the time, but we all kinda just…minded our own business—the humans and the non-humans. At least in the country I grew up in. But then the war started, so…."

She sighed a little. "Yeah. My family and I are no strangers to war and what it does to both people and the land." With a shake of her head, she smiled. "Anyway, I don't mean to dull the mood." She looked out the window. "It looks like we're getting close."

Danford looked out there, too, watching as the snowy landscape passed them by.

"I love the snow," Freja said. "It makes everything look so much prettier."

"I like the way it feels under my paws," he said, glancing down at his hands. "A-and how it glistens like stars when the morning light and moonlight hit it just right," he added shyly, smiling as he looked outside the carriage window again.

"Sitting inside a cave or under the cover of trees and watching it fall all around you," she said with a sigh. "The snow would get so thick in Dor-Sanguis that we'd practically have to swim through it at times."

"Was it tall enough to make mazes?" he asked.

"Sometimes when it got *really* cold," she said with a nod. "When I was a pup, my parents would make tunnels for my sisters and me, and we'd play around in them all night," she said with a quiet laugh, resting her hands in her lap. "I lost them in the war, though—my parents. We lost a lot of wolves in that war."

Danford didn't really know how to respond, so he just frowned sullenly and nodded.

"What were *your* parents like?" she asked, clearly trying to smile away her sadness.

"Very artsy and creative," he answered as the carriage turned and approached the city. "My mom had a million hobbies she'd use to make money, and my dad was a writer; he was obsessed with those ship-in-a-bottle things, too," he said with a light chuckle. "They were both human."

"Human?" she questioned, sounding surprised. "Did they adopt you?"

"Yeah. They found me as a baby abandoned in some bushes or something out behind their property line." It didn't make him sad to think about it, though. His parents were good to him, and he was happy that they took him in.

Freja frowned sympathetically. "I don't agree with that ideology… abandoning pups for any reason at all. That's your *child*." She then widened her eyes a little. "Sorry, I don't want to upset you."

He shrugged and said, "I like to think that my birth mother or whoever left me there because she knew that my parents would find me and take care of me. I'm happy with how things turned out in the end."

She smiled at him. "Well, your happiness is what matters, right?"

Danford nodded. "Yeah."

The carriage started slowing.

Freja opened the small window behind the coachman's seat. "It's just up here on the left," she told the man.

"Right away, ma'am," he replied.

She closed the window and smiled at Danford.

He smiled back nervously, and once the carriage stopped, he opened the door and let Freja climb out first. And when *he* stepped out, he was struck with surprise, taking in the scene before him. The streets weren't busy or loud or packed with drunks and shady figures as he had expected. Instead, they were gently alive, filled with the quiet hum of upper-class life. Well-dressed human and elf men and women strolled by, their polished shoes tapping softly against the snowy cobblestones, their conversations a hushed murmur in the cool evening air. There wasn't even the slightest scent of hostile wolves upon the breeze, so *that* calmed him a little…but he'd not let his guard down.

The buildings around him were a far cry from the usual taverns and pubs he frequented. Made of stone and marble, each one was grand and imposing, their facades gleaming under the soft glow of gas lamps. Some were even plated with gold accents, catching the light and reflecting it like precious jewels against the darkening sky. Ornate iron railings lined the streets, and carriages passed by, their wheels barely making a sound on the well-maintained road.

The entire street felt pristine, almost otherworldly, as if he'd wandered into a part of the city he had never known existed—a world of wealth and refinement, so different from the one he was used to navigating. It left him feeling slightly out of place yet intrigued by this glimpse into a life so distant from his own.

And then there was the bar. Most of the higher-ranking pack members preferred smaller, rougher pubs tucked away from the main streets, places where the atmosphere was gritty and unpolished. But this was different. Of course, it made sense that the Luna of the pack would choose somewhere far more refined. Unlike The Grey Goose or Ram's Hooves, this bar exuded sophistication. It looked clean, fancy, and undoubtedly expensive. Even the name—Rosemary Inn Restaurant and Bar—carried an air of elegance that was far removed from the usual haunts.

Inside, the bright, warm glow of chandeliers overhead greeted them as they stepped past the threshold. Danford blinked against the light, momentarily taken aback by the stark contrast to the dimly lit, smoky places he was used to. The interior was polished to a gleam, with dark, rich mahogany wood panelling lining the walls, creating a warm, intimate atmosphere. The bar itself was long and sleek, the marble countertop reflecting the glow of the amber lights overhead, while bottles of the finest liquors were displayed like trophies on the shelves behind.

The patrons matched the ambience—well-dressed men in tailored suits and women in elegant dresses, their laughter and conversations a soft murmur in the background. Plush leather chairs and finely upholstered booths were arranged throughout the space, giving the room a sense of comfort and exclusivity. The scent of roasted meats and freshly baked bread wafted through the air, mingling with the faint aroma of expensive cigars.

In the far corner, a grand piano played softly, adding a gentle melody to the atmosphere. It felt like stepping into a different world—a world of refinement, where every detail was meticulously crafted to exude class. Danford glanced at Freja, suddenly feeling out of place, but as her golden eyes sparkled with amusement, he realized this was exactly where she belonged. And for now, he was along for the ride.

"I know I asked before," Freja said, guiding him towards one of the booths, "but of all the people Aegisguard had to offer, why choose that aristocrat-wannabe Luther?"

Danford let out a deep sigh as he tried to make himself comfortable. "He was just…nice," he mumbled, trying to fight the nervousness keeping a tight hold around him. "He saw past the boring, quiet nobody, he was interested in my drawings, and he was easy to talk to." He exhaled deeply. "I mean…now that I think about and look back at it all, I know that he wasn't listening when I was ranting or pouring my heart out, but I guess made myself believe that he was."

Freja shook her head. "He doesn't deserve you, Danford." She waved a waitress over. "And to be honest, it's for the best. Vampires and werewolves never work out."

He chuckled sadly, looking down at his arms as he rested them on the table. "Yeah, I guess you're right about that. I kinda just thought he was different."

"Greymore tried to ward him off you, didn't he?" Freja asked. Then, she told the waitress, "I'll have a white wine, please. Danford?"

"Oh, uh…just um…a soda is fine—orange."

"Right away," the waitress said and wandered off.

Freja smiled across the table at him. "Where were we?"

"Greymore."

"Oh, yeah. He warded Luther off, right?"

"I mean…I guess that's what he tried to do. Maybe he sensed that something was up. He's always been good at that kind of thing."

She nodded, leaning back in her seat.

"I listened. I mean I left the table and eventually left the bar, too, but Luther found me."

"Of course he did," she said with a roll of her eyes.

As his nervousness grew under her intimidating gaze, Danford fiddled with his eyepatch and shuffled in his seat.

"How did that happen?" Freja asked curiously, pointing to her own left eye.

"Oh…" Danford mumbled, pulling his hand away from his patch. "We were all fighting the humans; it was a really big battle. They had gryphons and stuff, and one of them flew down behind me. I turned to face it, but it slashed the side of my face," he said, guiding his fingers over the side of his face where the wounds had once been. "My face healed, but my eye didn't. I mean it's still there…it's just…gross," he muttered and grimaced.

Freja adorned a devious smile and leaned closer to him, resting her arms on the table. "Can I see?"

Her request made him uncomfortable. He hated what his eye looked like, and he didn't want the state of it to disgust and potentially scare away the pack's Luna and someone who might actually become his friend. He didn't have many of those.

"Sorry," she said and laughed a little—was that… anxiety in her voice? "I get a little too forward sometimes. I get it from my mom."

Danford smiled as best he could through his confliction. "It's okay."

"Your drinks, ma'am, sir," came the waitress' voice. She placed their drinks down and then wandered off again.

Freja took a sip of her wine. "Mm. This place is my favourite. The wine is to die for." She held the glass towards him. "Want to try some?"

"Uh… sure," he said and took the glass from her. He sipped from it, and it was pretty good… for wine. "It's good," he said. And then he glanced down at his orange soda. "Do you um… wanna try some?"

She nodded, looking enthusiastic. "I've never tried soda," she said, taking the glass from him. The Luna took a sip, smiled, and handed it back to him. "It feels strange in your mouth… like vibrations, almost."

"The fizzing," he said with a nod. "It's the citric acid; it reacts with the carbonate in bicarbonate of the soda to form carbon dioxide gas," he explained matter-of-factly.

Freja looked surprised again. "You know your stuff, don't you?"

He shrugged again. "I read a lot sometimes."

"Just facts about fizzing drinks or fiction, too?"

"A little bit of both. I like learning what I can about this world… you know, since I live here now."

She smiled and said, "Some of the books you find here—especially in Nefastus—can be very misleading. The best history books I've peeked at were in Aleksei's library. Most of them were in Dor-Sanguian, though, so I'm not sure they'd be much use."

He nodded in response, sipping from his drink.

"I could tell you, though," she offered, and there it was again, that hint of shyness in her voice. "Only if you want, that is. What I know mostly revolves around werewolves, but I'm certain that some of it hasn't made it into any book."

Danford managed an awkward smile. "Yeah, thanks. That'd be cool."

She smiled at him, and he couldn't help but smile back, though his heart quickened as their eyes met across the table. For a moment, everything else seemed to fade away, leaving only the quiet space between them. Her golden eyes shimmered in the dim light, and something about them sent a shiver down Danford's spine—an unexplainable chill that both unsettled and captivated him. It was as if her gaze held him in place, wrapping him in a strange blend of nervousness and enchantment.

He didn't understand why he felt this way. There was something magnetic about her presence, something that stirred an eagerness in him that he couldn't quite explain. He wanted to know more—about her, about her family, about the past that shaped her. Questions burned at the edge of his mind, a growing curiosity he couldn't suppress. Yet, despite the growing desire to know everything about her, he felt a quiet desperation to keep those questions hidden. She was still his Alpha, after all, and the last thing he wanted was to overstep, to risk prying too far and upsetting her.

And yet, the pull was undeniable. Every glance and every smile only deepened the sense that there was something more beneath the surface, something he was desperate to uncover. But for now, all he could do was sit there, trapped in her gaze, uncertain of why he felt this way, or why the need for more seemed to press so urgently against his chest.

"Anyway," she said, abruptly breaking their locked gaze and the serene silence. "This whole um…Greymore thing," she said.

Danford sipped from his drink. He wasn't sure what thing she was referring to, but he'd listen and wait.

"We're not…well, it's not…*real*," she said, looking a little confounded. "It's just business. We're not mated, marked, any of the real stuff."

He nodded stiffly. "Y-yeah, I know."

"And it's kinda hard, you know? No one wants to date the married Luna," she said with a sigh. "I mean I was seeing one guy—uh…Phillip."

"Oh, Phil is nice," Danford said with a nod. "He's very good at archery."

"Yeah, he took me one weekend to an archery range just outside the city."

Danford fiddled with his eyepatch again, nervous to ask his next question. "So, uh…what happened?"

Freja sighed deeply. "It ended the same way all my attempts at dating have lately. I beat him at archery, and he told me that he couldn't date a woman more powerful than him." She scoffed. "What is it with men and that damn power dynamic? Why can't a woman have a successful career while he stays at home and watches the kids?"

He laughed a little. "I guess…well…maybe it's just an ego thing."

She smiled, but sadness lingered in her eyes. "Yeah. I suppose I just have to keep searching for that odd one percent, huh?"

"I suppose."

Freja sipped from her drink. "I imagine it's not so different for you, huh?"

"Uh…what do you mean?"

"Well, you date men, too, so I imagine that a lot of them are the same in that sense. Power dynamics, etcetera."

He shook his head. "I mean…some, sure. A lot of them just want to screw around, though. It's hard to find a man who wants to settle down." And then the nervousness returned. "I don't just…date men, though," he said, fiddling with his eyepatch. "I see women, too."

Freja's eyes widened slightly—perhaps with surprise. "Oh…so, you're bisexual?"

"Yeah."

"Do you like…have a preference?"

"Not really," he said with a shrug. "I like who I like, you know?"

She smiled and said, "So, how many women have you dated?"

Danford chuckled shyly, looking down at his drink. "Not many. I haven't dated many men, either, actually." He exhaled deeply, thinking back. "My first girlfriend was Leocadia Hawkins. She came with her pack to this sort of…exchange. The wolf packs would meet and exchange members every year at the beginning of winter, and my parents let me attend when I was sixteen."

Freja nodded. "We do that here, too."

He smiled slightly in response and then continued, "She had this really long, blonde, curly hair. I guess we thought we were meant for each other because we both felt this sort of…spark when we first saw one other. But a few months in, we learned more about each other, and we decided that it wasn't meant to be. She'd also been seeing one of the Betas behind my back, so…yeah," he mumbled.

The Luna tutted. "Even the women can't stay loyal."

Danford laughed a little. "To be fair, it was hard to bond. I lived in this fancy human cottage while she roamed the woods. Seeing each other got harder and harder because her pack were expanding their territory, and crossing the river was dangerous, too."

"Did Leocadia come to Aegisguard?" Freja asked curiously.

"No. I never saw her again after we broke up, or any of her pack. I don't know if she's still out there somewhere or if…well, if she's gone," he said with a despondent sigh. "I admittedly still think about them all sometimes—all the wolves who might still be out there. Zalith and Greymore tried their best to find as many as they could, but they had to stop searching when things got *really* bad."

Freja slowly reached her hand across the table and placed it over his. "I know how hard it must have all been."

Danford tensed, a ripple of unease and shock surging through him at the light brush of Freja's touch. He never would've expected someone like her to invite him out for drinks, let alone to touch him so casually. It was something so far beyond his imagination that, even in this moment, it felt unreal—like a fleeting dream he never thought he'd experience.

She pulled her hand back and sipped from her wine. "What about your first boyfriend? Was it Zalith?"

He laughed softly. "No. My first boyfriend was Emory Mercer of the Mercer Estate," he said with a fond smile.

"Ooh, a rich boy?" she asked with a smirk.

"Yeah, one of the richest, actually. I met him when I was up in the richer parts of the city delivering an order with my mom. She'd made this beautiful rug using the fur of a bear, and it was for Mrs Mercer. My mom told me to wait in the carriage, but me being the curious teenager I was back then, I got out to look at all the carved hedges. One of them looked like this big dragon," he explained, holding out his arms to show her just how big it was. "There were so many fine details—I was fascinated."

"Like those ones in Zalith and Aleksei's garden?"

He nodded. "Yeah, animals and stuff. Anyway, I was looking at this dragon hedge, and then I heard someone curse. I peeked around the hedge, and there he was. Emory was smoking one of his dad's cigarettes; apparently, behind the dragon hedge was the only place he could hide because his dad once found a nest of spiders inside the branches and didn't want to go anywhere near it ever again," he laughed.

Freja laughed, too. "Spiders are such... ghastly little things."

Danford smiled again. "Emory didn't mind them—in fact, he had a pet tarantula."

"Oh, God," the Luna grimaced, shaking her head.

"Anyway, Emory was completely startled, and he begged me not to tattle. I told him I wouldn't. We kinda just got to talking and found out that we had a lot in common, and when it was time for me to go, he invited me to have lunch the next day." That was when his fond smile faded. "We were together a while; I guess I was the one who helped Emory understand his sexuality, which I mean... I don't mind; everyone needs their discovery. But when we were talking about telling our parents about our relationship, Emory told me that he was a member of the Frostfang Pack."

Freja looked intrigued. "What was wrong with the Frostfang Pack?"

"They were extremely hostile towards rogues, and that was what I was until Zalith told me to join Greymore's pack. I knew Greymore for a long time before I joined the pack, though, and I did odd jobs here and there for Zalith." He paused and sighed. "Anyway, Emory and I could never be together, not unless he left the pack; if he did that, though, he'd lose his family name, and with it, the money. So—"

"He chose the money and status over you."

Danford pouted sadly. "Yeah."

She sighed and shook her head. "You were better off without him. We should all be equal and a first priority to each other in a relationship."

He nodded and said, "But finding someone who feels that way is starting to seem impossible."

"It is," she agreed and finished her wine. She then waved the waitress over to fetch her another.

Danford sipped from his drink and fiddled with his eyepatch. He didn't want the conversation to end, but his nervousness restricted him from asking a single question.

"All of my sisters are married," Freja suddenly said. "*Actually* married, not fake married like Greymore and me. My youngest sister, Sophronia, mated with and married Llewellyn from the pack that belonged to Tobias—I don't know if you know about him."

He nodded. "Yeah, I... I heard the stories."

"Well, she's pregnant now; they'd been trying for a year-ish," Freja said; although every word she spoke remained a reel pulling Danford in, the sadness in her voice was getting deeper. "My second youngest sister, Opal, she's marrying Roscoe next month."

"Oh, Roscoe is a good guy," Danford assured her.

"They knew from the moment they saw each other that they were fated," she said longingly. "And then my third youngest sister, Verity...she found Imogene. *All* my sisters have their mates. And I don't know if being married to Greymore will prevent me from finding mine forever, or if...maybe this business marriage is some kinda weird game that the Moon Goddess is playing with me. But when I think about him being my fated mate, I get this...sickly feeling—not sick, but like...anxious, nauseous."

Danford was surprised to hear that since everyone seemed to love Greymore. In response, though, he nodded and said, "No, I understand. It's that feeling of...feeling like you're going to have to settle for something you don't want."

"Exactly. Greymore isn't my type *at all*, and I don't see either of us growing on each other." She scoffed amusedly and said, "When he was drunk as hell one night, he told me that he finds me too...controlling."

He frowned as he sipped from his soda. "You don't...seem controlling to me."

"I think it's because I always told him to stop snoring or stop eating like a pig in his human form or stop spending so much time in the bar.

"Well, I guess Greymore never really did like being told what to do...other than by his boss...*bosses*."

Freja shrugged as her drink arrived. "Well, I guess he doesn't have to worry about dealing with me as his actual wife." She put her drink down and said to the waitress, "Thank you."

Danford took a few more sips of his soda. "Did you...see anyone before Greymore?" he asked, finally finding the courage.

The Luna laughed a little and drank her wine. "No. I was waiting for that spark, that little bit intense pull of fate, you know?"

"I wish I *did* know it," he mumbled.

"I never really saw the point in dating someone if they weren't my fated partner. I mean I get why some people do it...the loneliness and companionship and all that. But I could never quite grasp that."

Danford nodded, frowning sadly. "It *does* get very lonely."

"Who knows?" she pondered. "Maybe once Greymore has made treaties with all these other packs around here, I'll...go to one of those exchanges, join some other pack. Maybe the men are better out there."

He chuckled lightly. "Yeah, maybe. I might even do the same."

She lifted her eyes from her glass, locking her gaze on him. "Are you going to be waiting for Luther to come home tonight?"

The question hit him like a red-hot blade, slicing through the fragile defences he'd tried to build around his heart. He already knew the answer but saying it aloud would make it hurt even more. For a moment, his throat tightened, but he forced the words out, each one stinging. "No," he muttered, his voice strained. "I know he's…he's staying with Varana." The admission felt like twisting the knife, the pain sharper now that it had been spoken aloud.

"Hmm," Freja responded and sipped from her wine. "Are you going to break it off with him?"

He sighed deeply, the pain growing with each passing moment. "I don't know," he mumbled. He wasn't sure he'd be strong enough—he wasn't even entirely sure whether he wanted to, but…he knew that he should.

"You deserve so much better, Danford."

With a shake of his head, a pout, and a sip of his drink, he looked away to hide his distressed frown. "I know, I just…it's…hard, and—"

"Put him out of your mind for now," Freja interjected. "It's Yule. We're supposed to be having fun, right? I'm sorry I asked."

He exhaled deeply. "It's okay." With his best smile, he then asked, "Do you have plans for tomorrow?"

She shrugged, dragging her finger around the rim of her glass. "No. You?"

Danford held his tongue. He remembered Luther's words, but he was almost certain that he'd make up some kind of excuse. So he sadly said, "Probably not."

Freja smiled, but there was nervousness in her eyes. "So, it wouldn't matter if we got drunk and slept in, would it?" she giggled.

He froze up for a moment, unsure of what she meant. But he didn't want to assume, so he laughed with her. "Yeah, I guess it wouldn't."

She finished her drink and slid her hand across the table. As she stroked her fingertips over his knuckles, she murmured, "So…should we go back to your room?"

That was when Danford became so flustered that his entire body tensed, and his heart thumped *hard*. His mind raced, and he had no idea what to say; all he could do was sit there and stare at Freja, red-faced and entirely absorbed by startle, confusion, and embarrassment. Freja…the pack *Luna* was asking him if he wanted to take her back to his room. Was this actually happening? Or was he having some sort of hallucination, some kind of psychosis caused by the heartbreak of Luther's constant betrayal?

But as he stared across the table at her, time ticked back into place, and he realized that he really was sitting across the table from her, that she really was touching his hand, and that she really had just asked him to go back to his room.

What was he supposed to say?

Did he *want* to go back to his room with her?

He thought about it, and the idea made him feel guilty. Even though she wasn't actually Greymore's wife or mate, he couldn't help but ask himself whether taking her back with him was wrong. *Was* it wrong? Should he figure out how to politely decline?

Did he want to decline?

Danford exhaled, trying to fight the confliction. No. Despite still feeling like things were moving at lightning speed, he didn't want to say no. Something inside him…his instincts, maybe…began *urging* him towards her. It pleaded that he said yes. After all, he wanted to know more about her, he wanted to get closer. Why would he turn away the chance?

Should he?

He looked down at her fingers as they brushed the back of his hand. Each stroke sent a wave of anticipation through him, urging him harder, pleading him with so much more desperation. And he let the words slip from his trembling lips, "Okay."

Chapter Three

>—) 𝕯 (—«

Connection

An overwhelming flurry of emotions raced through Danford as Freja led them from the building and through the snowy streets. His heart was racing, his legs were trembling, and his thoughts were spiralling around inside his head like a whirlwind. At the same time, he felt the conflicting concoction of desperation to find out where this would lead and the confusion as to why it was all moving so fast. *Why* was Freja so insistent?

He let the doubt creep in for a moment. What if this was some kind of prank? A dare? What if her friends were waiting back on the ship to greet him with hysterical laughs and horrible points? Or what if she was using him to make someone else jealous? What if she was using him to prove to her sisters that she wasn't incapable of seducing a man? Or what if she was using him as some sort of experiment? A stepping stone to finding her mate where waiting had failed her?

And then there was Greymore. The last thing he wanted to do was piss him off. What if Greymore wouldn't appreciate him hanging around with his wife? What if Greymore found out that they spent tonight together…that they…had sex? Would he scold him? Yell at him? …Worse?

Danford's already tense body shivered as his nervousness grew, and when he saw that they'd reached the shipyard, his anxiety intensified so much that his breath caught in his throat, and he struggled to find both the words and thoughts to act upon. He knew why they were going back to his room, and he was certain he knew what was going to happen. Was it so awful of him to want it? Was he a horrible, atrocious person for wanting to continue following Freja as she led him up onto the galleon and towards the door that led below deck?

The eagerness gnawed at him, overtaking the confliction swirling in his chest. He couldn't resist her, and despite the doubts clawing at the back of his mind, he followed Freja below deck. When she asked where his room was, he led her without hesitation, his heart pounding with anticipation. As soon as the door clicked shut behind them, there was no time for second thoughts—Freja didn't even wait for him to light the lanterns. She grabbed his arms and pushed him firmly against the wooden wall, her breath warm and quick against his face, an excited smile tugging at her lips.

Danford's own nerves shot through him like electricity, but it was her who was trembling slightly. Even in the dark, he could see the flicker of nervousness in her eyes, yet she didn't hesitate. Her lips were on his in an instant, the kiss sending a rush of heat through his body. His heart raced even faster, pounding in sync with the wine-tinged taste of her kiss. Her movements were fast, almost frantic, her hands trailing down his chest and his stomach as if she couldn't get enough of him. Desperation coursed through her touch, and it made him dizzy with desire and confusion all at once.

But with each touch, each kiss, the doubts crept in. Why was she here? Why was she so insistent? Anxiety twisted in his gut. Was she using him? Playing with him just because she could? The thought gnawed at him, but the way her body pressed against his, the heat of her skin under his fingers…it drowned out his doubts.

Not his hesitation, though.

When Freja leaned in to kiss him again, he unsurely placed his hand on her shoulder. "Um…are you…sure this is okay?" he asked shakily.

"It's fine," she insisted, her voice a hushed snap. But a frown then struck her face. "Do you not want to?"

His instincts urged him, and he let them influence his answer. "N-no, I do, I just…don't want to do something that's gonna piss Greymore off."

Freja smiled and rolled her eyes. "Greymore doesn't give a fuck." She started unbuttoning his shirt. "He's probably wandered off with his own girl by now."

"O-oh…o-okay—"

She pressed her lips against his, silencing him, and this time, he slowly and nervously kissed back. Shivers spiraled through him as she stroked her hands over his bare chest, and when her fingertips edged nearer to his crotch, the uncertainty returned.

"I-I mean, are you totally—"

"I'm totally sure, Danford," she said firmly, unbuckling and pulling his belt from around his waist. Then, she got down on her knees.

Danford bit back a startled yet utterly pleased moan as Freja's lips brushed over the tip of his hardening dick. The sensation sent a jolt of pleasure up his spine, making him lean his head back against the wall, his eyes closing. Every slow, deliberate drag of her tongue along his shaft pulled him deeper into the moment, unravelling the tension that had kept his heart fluttering with nervousness. But as Freja found her rhythm, the pleasure steadily overtook the anxiety, melting it away.

A quiet groan escaped his lips as he tentatively placed his hand on her head, his fingers weaving into the soft curls of her golden hair. The gentle pressure of his touch matched the slow, sensual pace she had set. There was no rush, no impatience in her movements—just a steady, deliberate attention that sent waves of heat pulsing through him. It felt different, so different from what he was used to. With Luther, it had always felt rushed, mechanical—like something to get over with. But this... this was different.

No. He didn't want to think about *him*.

Danford inhaled sharply, letting out a low groan as he forced thoughts of Luther out of his mind. He focused on the here and now—the soft caress of Freja's lips, the way her tongue teased him, how she seemed to want *him* in a way he hadn't felt in so long. His hand drifted down, brushing the side of her face, fingers tracing the curve of her jaw with a gentle touch.

When his hand reached her chin, he softly urged her to rise. Freja slowly stood, wiping her lips with the back of her hand, her eyes meeting his with a hint of nervousness. That vulnerability in her gaze made Danford's heart flutter in a different way, and he couldn't help but smile back at her, shyly. The tension in the air shifted as she kissed him, a hungry, desperate kiss that made him forget everything but her.

As they kissed, her hands gripped his arms, pulling him toward the bed. Her fingers worked hastily, unbuttoning her blouse, revealing more of her skin with each movement. Danford's breath quickened, the anticipation growing stronger with every second, his mind consumed by her—by the heat of her body against his, by the way her hands moved, eager and unashamed.

He helped her out of her dress, and once she was free, she fell back onto his bed, pulling him with her. Danford took his trousers off and positioned himself comfortably over her, and when her hands graced the sides of his face, he leaned closer and kissed her lips. The desperation for more was quickly becoming overwhelming, but he didn't want to rush. For just a few more moments, they kissed, and then Danford shyly pulled his face away from hers and kissed her neck, her collarbone, and what of her chest wasn't concealed by her corset.

Danford listened to Freja's frantic, anticipation-filled breaths as he unlaced her corset; of course, he felt shy about pulling it off, but she did it for him. She then gripped his wrist and made him place his hand over her right breast, but he was afraid that he might hurt her or do something wrong, so he didn't grip so hard, he just squeezed it lightly while he gently sucked on her other nipple, making her hum quietly in content.

And then he made his slow descent, kissing his way down her body. She flinched ever so lightly with each press of his lips, and when he reached her legs, he carefully gripped and spread her thighs before dragging his tongue over her clit. Freja moaned quietly in delight, tensing in his gentle grip. She tasted sweet, like honey and warmth. Danford's lips hovered over her for a moment, savouring the way her body responded to him. He dragged his tongue over her clit again, slower this time, his own anticipation building as he felt her tense beneath his touch. Freja's quiet moan sent a shiver through him, her thighs trembling ever so slightly in his gentle grip.

The sound of her pleasure, soft but undeniable, made Danford's heart race even faster. He could feel the desperation rising in him, that gnawing urge to lose himself in her completely. But he didn't rush—not yet. He wanted this to last. He wanted every breath, every movement to be deliberate, to show her that he was there, with her, in this moment.

Freja's hand reached down, threading into his hair, and he felt a small tug as her hips shifted, pressing toward him. He took the cue, flicking his tongue against her again, this time with more pressure, and her soft hum of approval made his pulse quicken. The taste of her, the feel of her skin beneath his lips—it was intoxicating, overwhelming, and Danford couldn't stop himself from wanting more.

He kissed his way back up her body, appreciating the feel of her beneath him, her breath quickening with each touch. Her hands moved over his back, tracing lines up to his shoulders, and the heat between them felt almost unbearable. But even in his eagerness, he wanted her to guide him, to be sure of what she wanted from him, and as he reached her lips again, she pulled him closer, her kiss deep and urgent, telling him everything he needed to know.

The desire to please her, to prove that he was more than the insecure mess he often felt like fuelled him. He moved his hand back to her breast, this time with more confidence, the softness of her skin against his fingers grounding him. Freja's breath hitched, and her body arched into his touch, making him feel something he hadn't in a long time—wanted, needed. And for now, in the heat of this moment, that was everything.

Freja's fingertips drifted down his body with a slow, deliberate touch that sent waves of anticipation through him. When her hand finally found his dick, she wrapped her fingers around him with an eager grip that made his breath catch. With a soft hum of need, she hooked one leg over his back, pulling him closer, guiding him toward her. Danford's heart pounded, and he didn't want to disappoint her.

As she urged him forward, he slowly eased his dick inside her, the sensation overwhelming as her warm, wet pussy enveloped him. The tightness of her walls gripped him inch by inch, drawing him deeper. They both moaned, the sound mingling in the thick air between them as he pushed gently, savouring every moment of that slow, sweet descent. The heat of her body surrounded him, and Danford had to take a deep breath to keep himself from losing control too quickly.

Freja's back arched beneath him, her hands gripping his shoulders as if to pull him even closer. The way she moved against him—desperate and wanting—fuelled his need, but he kept his pace steady. He wanted to feel every second of this, every breathless moment of her warmth around him, every inch that brought them closer together.

Her quiet gasps, her body reacting to his every movement sent shockwaves of pleasure coursing through him. He buried himself deeper, groaning softly as he felt her walls tighten around him, her leg pressing against his back urging him to go further. The connection between them, the way her body clung to his... it was intoxicating. He couldn't hold back the low groan that escaped him as he pulled her hips closer, delving into her warmth, wanting—*needing*—to give her everything in that moment.

Danford slowly pulled back, the friction sending a wave of pleasure through him, and then he gently pushed back in, his quiet hum of contentment blending with Freja's soft, breathless gasp. He was deliberate, careful not to go too fast or be too rough, the last remnants of his confliction keeping him grounded. His movements were slow, controlled, each careful thrust causing her to tighten around him, her body responding in kind.

But when Freja's fingers tangled in his hair, gripping a fistful and pulling his face closer to hers, the connection between them deepened. She kissed him hard, her lips hungry with desperation, and he felt his restraint slipping. The heat of her kiss urged him on, pushing him to thrust a little faster, a little deeper. Her moans grew louder, each sound pulling him further into the moment, into her.

Their kisses became frantic, tongues entwining as deep breaths mingled between them. With each thrust, Danford felt her body arch against his, her nails scraping lightly against his back as their rhythm built together. The soft gasps and moans escaping Freja's lips drove him wild, every sound urging him to give her more. He lost himself in the taste of her, the way her body moved beneath his, and the way their breaths and heartbeats seemed to synchronize in the heat of it all.

Every touch, every kiss felt like it burned with the same intensity as the desperation they both shared, and as their lips met again and again, Danford couldn't help but feel himself sinking deeper into her—not just physically, but emotionally, the connection between them more powerful than he ever imagined.

And that was when he felt it.

The connection... it was unlike anything he'd ever imagined. Something deeper, more powerful than he'd ever thought possible. His instincts flared, primal and raw as the wolf inside him stirred, pleading for Freja's touch, begging for her acceptance. With every second that passed, the desperation in him swelled, his need growing stronger, almost unbearable. The longing, the desire—it consumed him.

He tried to focus on his movements, to keep his mind on the beautiful, intoxicating woman beneath him. The way her body responded to his, the way her moans seemed to urge him forward. But he struggled. The pull was overwhelming, magnetic, as if an invisible force was drawing him closer to her soul, deeper into something he couldn't quite grasp. It was as if she could devour him entirely, and if she did, he would surrender willingly.

This pull...it was telling him something. Something that sent a shock of disbelief through him, a feeling so profound it made him question his own sanity. Was this real? Was he just imagining it, conjuring this out of a deep-rooted desire he'd long buried, the desire to finally feel what others in the pack had spoken of—the unmistakable bond that only fated mates could share?

But no. This was different. It wasn't a dream or a fantasy.

Freja wasn't just the pack's Luna.

No...to Danford, Freja was something much more. Something he'd never dared to hope for.

Freja was his fated mate.

A confused, conflicted frown broke through his pleased expression, but he couldn't process it. His body tensed, urging him to thrust into Freja a little faster. Freja suddenly moaned loudly, almost whining as she arched her body upwards, her tight walls throbbing around Danford's dick as she climaxed. And he followed moments later, reaching his peak, tipping over the edge—

He pulled out, moaning in both relief and satisfaction as he came *hard*, a climax that didn't feel rushed or like a long-awaited, inconvenient end. The pleasure spiralled through him, and a content hum sat on each exhale. He opened his eyes, meeting Freja's euphoric gaze, and as he stared into her golden eyes, the overwhelming desire of their connection struck him. Did she feel it too? That pull...that desperation. He couldn't tell, but he wouldn't dare ask.

With a deep exhale, he grabbed his shirt and used it to clean up before he moved off her and laid down beside her, his trembling body gradually calming. But the wolf inside him didn't settle. It clawed at his skin, *begging* him to seek the same feeling within Freja, urging him to mark, to mate, to claim.

"Are you okay?" Freja asked, her voice carrying not only relief...but...concern?

Danford nodded. "Y-yeah. Are you?"

She smiled as she turned onto her side and leaned up on her arm, looking down at him. "Yeah," she replied, her eyes looking him up and down.

He felt nervous, completely exposed to her sights; she eyed him as if she were deciding whether she wanted to savour or devour, a predator torn between kindness and its true nature. Danford resisted the urge to pull the blanket over himself because he didn't want to make her mad. If she wanted to examine every inch of his body, he'd let her. Not only because he was afraid of upsetting her, but also because he felt the desire to cave under her silent commands. That connection...it urged him to give himself to her completely; it urged him to let her decide whether she wanted to accept...or reject. So he lay there...waiting under her gaze.

But then she laid down, resting her head on the pillow. "Is it okay if I sleep here tonight?" she asked quietly. The concern in her voice was gone; now, it was nervousness.

Danford nodded, surprised that she wasn't planning on immediately leaving. "Y-yeah, of course."

She smiled and kissed his cheek. Then, she grabbed the blanket and pulled it over them both. She turned her back to him, though, resting on her right side.

He glanced at her, and he saw the pack mark on her back—a lily-like flower against a full moon. It was a little darker than her tanned skin and could easily be mistaken for a natural birthmark—unless... *that* was what it was.

Danford didn't want to stare, though. He turned his head to look up at the ceiling. As the pleasure of his climax faded, the confliction and confounding thoughts flooded in like a tsunami. What he felt was *real*. That pull, that tugging, yearning connection. But his disbelief kept him from uttering a word about it. It couldn't be... could it? Him... a loser, a nobody... fated to a *Luna*? He couldn't be. He *shouldn't* be. Maybe he was confusing his attraction to her for that fated pull.

No. His wolf told him *no*. It *was* real. The woman beside him... it was *her*.

But then came the fear, the sickly doubt, the nauseating wonder. Had she felt it too? What if she had and was considering whether or not she wanted him? What if *that* was why she was looking him up and down... determining if he was enough or not? He scowled anxiously, glancing at her again. Would she reject him? Would she plunge that harsh, sharp dagger through his already broken heart? He wasn't sure he could handle it. The pain... the embarrassment.

He exhaled quietly, closing his eyes in an attempt to silence his thoughts. Freja was a Luna, an *Alpha*. If she *had* felt the fated pull... of course she'd need time to think about it, to consider her options, her duties, and the results of whatever choice she'd make. All Danford could do was wait. He wouldn't dare ask her about it. He wouldn't dare urge her for her choice. No, he'd just... wait.

But how long would Freja take to tell him if she wanted him... or rejected him?

Chapter Four

>→) 🦇 (→«

Gone

| *Saturday, Clausula 31*, *959(TG)—Nefastus* |

The gentle sway of the boat slowly pulled Danford from his sleep. Sunlight shone in through the cracks in the beige curtains, and the smell of cooking breakfast wafted through the ship. He heard everyone laughing and chatting, enjoying the last day of Yule, but he didn't have any plans—not really. Luther was probably still with Varana since he hadn't turned up in the early hours of the morning like he usually did.

But then he remembered—Freja.

He rolled onto his back as he moved his hand around, feeling for her…but the other side of his bed was empty. Freja was gone; all that remained were two of her long, curly golden hairs and her sweet, ginger-like scent. He sat up, looking around his room, but he didn't find the Luna, nor did he find a note. She was just…gone.

Danford frowned sullenly, and his heart hurt. But he wasn't surprised, and he felt silly for being sad about it. This was obviously going to happen. Why would she want *him*? Why would *anyone* want him?

But…that feeling, that desperation, that connection….

No. Maybe he was mistaken. Maybe he just wanted what he felt to be the pull of fate because Freja was beautiful, because she talked to him like he was a person, and because she'd actually shown some interest. But she'd only wanted him for one thing…and that was okay. It wasn't the first time, and it wouldn't be the last. He just hoped that he wouldn't be pointed and laughed at because it *had* been a joke or a dare.

With a deep, sullen sigh, he got out of bed and went over to his dresser—

A quiet, squeaking groan broke the silence.

Danford flinched. "Oh, my fff…" he dragged the letter out as his startled frown located an izuret. It lay on the floor in the fruitcake box that Idina had left on his table, and it had eaten the *entire* thing. It looked sick, one hand on its swollen stomach and the other on its head. "Did you eat *all* of that?" he exclaimed.

The creature responded with a breathy groan of confirmation.

He sighed deeply. That was his *only* Yule gift…and now it was gone. "Just don't throw up in my room, please."

It groaned again, and it was clearly drunk; it managed to slowly form words, and it told him that…Luther had been sentenced by the Vampire Council and was locked up because…he assaulted Aleksei?

Danford frowned in confusion. "What?"

And then it told him that Luther had *sexually* assaulted Aleksei.

"*What?!*" he exclaimed, unable to believe what he was hearing. He didn't want to believe it, but it was Zalith's message, and he trusted him more than Luther; he wouldn't make something like that up.

And that made Danford feel sick, disgusted—to think he'd let that kind of man touch him and flirt with him and make him feel like he meant something. His confusion boiled into revolt, anger. All the heartache and feelings of never being good enough were one thing, but this? He wished he'd never met Luther. He wished he had a way of deleting every memory of him from his mind.

With a sickly grimace, he laid back in bed and stared up at the ceiling. The disgust clashed with the returning weight of Freja's absence, though—her disappearance. He still wasn't surprised by the fact that she'd left without a word, but the more time passed by, the more it hurt. Hearing everyone above and around him having fun with their friends and family didn't help, either. It was all just a greater reminder that he was alone and probably always would be, good for nothing but time-passing and one-night stands.

He didn't want to lay there thinking about her, though. The night was over, and so was whatever they had. Instead, he looked across his small room at the izuret, which had managed to sit up inside the cake box. "Do you think that people are gonna think I'm like Luther?" he asked it.

The drunk creature blinked slowly and eventually told him that it didn't think so; a lot of people knew that Luther was using him.

His eyes widened. "Really? People talk about me?" he groaned embarrassedly.

It nodded.

"*Why?*" he drawled, almost whining. He hoped that no one saw him with Freja; he didn't want to deal with the gossip, and he didn't want her to be embarrassed about being seen with him…if they'd ever cross paths again.

What if *she* thought he was like Luther?

He dragged his hands over his face, overwhelmed with frustration, disgust, dismay, anger, and confusion. Before he could let any emotion overpower him, though, a knock came at his door, making him flinch. "One min," he called as he got up. He grabbed some clothes from the dresser and got dressed; he grabbed his cologne and sprayed it not only on himself but around his room, too, trying to hide any of Freja's lingering scent—the last thing he wanted was questions. Once he was done, he opened the door, and when he saw that it was Greymore, he tensed up, and fear raced through him. "Uh…" he drawled, wide-eyed. He hoped he couldn't smell Freja on him or in the room.

Greymore frowned a little. "Why do you look so suspicious?"

"I'm not," he replied, opening his door wider to show that he wasn't hiding anything.

For a moment, Greymore looked around, but he was quickly satisfied. "Okay. Upstairs," he said and walked down the corridor. "Happy Yule. We have shit to do."

Danford straightened himself up, pulled his door shut behind him, and followed after Greymore. They silently walked through the ship, heading towards the bar, where the sound of music and laughter grew louder. It wasn't until they were moments away that Greymore looked over his shoulder at him.

"Don't worry, I told everyone to leave you alone about the Luther getting locked up thing, by the way—assuming you know by now…hoping this isn't how you find out."

"An izuret told me a few minutes ago," he told him.

"Oh…."

"Is Aleksei okay? The izuret didn't leave out any details," he mumbled.

"Yeah, from what I've heard. It seems like we're the only two who know the full extent of what happened, though, so we best keep it to ourselves, yeah?"

Danford nodded, more than happy to keep it to himself. "Yeah."

They stopped at the end of the corridor and didn't continue right towards the bar.

"Why do you smell like Freja?" Greymore asked amusedly, but there was a little aggravation on his face.

He tensed up but did his best to hide his anxiety. "I was kinda sweaty with sweat because of anxiety or something and I bumped into her on my way out of the party, so I guess her scent clung to me or something," he replied, laughing a little.

Greymore raised an eyebrow but didn't respond.

"I actually think I forgot something in my room," Danford then said, his heart beating a little faster. "I'll be right back." He then hurriedly headed back towards his room. He was nervous as hell, and he didn't want to seem suspicious because people were going to ask a million questions. But then he thought about Freja again—what if she was at the party? His anxiety intensified, leaving him a trembling wreck as he stepped into his room and closed the door loudly behind him.

The izuret was *still* in the fruitcake box. It chirped at him, asking if he could help it up onto the bed.

With a deep, shaky sigh, he walked over there and helped the izuret up. He watched it make itself comfortable, and then he went into the bathroom. Once he pulled his clothes and eyepatch off, he climbed into the shower and switched the water on.

But as the water washed away Freja's scent from his skin, the dismay grew. It felt like he was peeling away a part of himself, like he was ridding himself of any remnant he had left of her. And he felt stupid for feeling that way because he was almost certain that what he felt last night wasn't a tug of fate but merely his own lonely, pathetic self yearning for that deep, eternal connection.

He exhaled deeply, trying to ignore the sadness, but it just got worse. Despite so many people before her using and leaving him, he just couldn't shake Freja. The thought of her clung to him like a tick, sapping away any other thought or emotion; all he could wonder while he stood under the water was where she had gone, who she was with, and if he'd ever get to talk to her again. But he doubted that he'd like the answer to any of those questions.

A heavy, despondent sigh left his lips as he switched the water off and climbed out of the shower. The drowning feeling of loneliness coiling around his heart was getting tighter the more he thought about Freja, the more he thought about last night. Why was he letting it get to him so much? Why couldn't he put her out of his mind? Even thinking about Luther didn't help. Nothing did, not even the atrocious thing that had gotten Luther locked up. No, his thoughts were just Freja, Freja, Freja.

He pulled his clothes and eyepatch on, doused himself in more cologne, and left the izuret to sleep, heading for the bar. The thought of seeing her among the crowd did relieve some of the pain, but it worsened the anxiety. He was afraid of *how* she might look at him if she glanced his way. Would she go to him? Talk to him? He wasn't sure, but he wasn't expecting anything.

And when he stepped into the bar, his observant eye didn't find the golden-eyed, blonde-haired Luna. Among the laughing, chatting, excited crowd, he found only his packmates. They were all enjoying themselves, hanging around with their friends and family, drinking eggnog, eating cookies and cake, and opening gifts while a band played a jolly tune in the background.

But there *he* was…alone. No friends to joke with, no family to open gifts with.

Danford was used to it, though. It had always been this way since he lost his parents. At least he was surrounded by his packmates; at least he wasn't left alone in silence. However, although he liked his fellow wolves, and although they liked him, he felt like he was still finding his place, like he didn't fit in here, and that hindered the enjoyment of being involved in pack celebrations. Would he ever find his place? He wasn't sure, but he'd keep looking.

He made his way to the bar and ordered a glass of eggnog, and then he sat there, watching as everyone else danced and celebrated. He'd join in if he was asked, but sitting there observing was what he was best at. And he was going to have to get used to being alone again since Luther was gone. But he wouldn't struggle. Most of his life after his parents' deaths had been spent alone, so he'd adjust. He just wished he didn't have to.

Chapter Five

⤛) 🜚 (⤜

Territory

As the afternoon carried on, Danford remained at the bar while his packmates partied around him. Sure, the odd person came over to tell him 'Happy Yule', but nobody lingered for a conversation. Still, that was to be expected. None of them really talked to him, not for longer than a few words or a sentence or two if he was lucky.

Of course, though, his mind lingered on Freja. He couldn't get her out of his head, and it was making him feel even lonelier than he already did. All the whys and what ifs flooded his mind, making his heart hurt, and when he finished his drink, he decided that maybe sleeping it off would help.

But just as he got up, Greymore stopped in front of him and firmly said, "Step outside the bar."

Danford tensed up again. Did Greymore know about Freja? Was he about to yell at him—*scream* at him? His heart raced, and he nodded nervously. "Uh…okay," he stammered and headed through the bustling crowd towards the door.

When he stepped outside the bar, though, he wasn't the only one in the hall. Ambrose, one of Greymore's two Betas, was there, along with Enforcers Edward, Clara, Louisa, and Lemuel. Etas Solomon and Althea were there, too. Was Greymore sending them on a hunt? A scouting mission, perhaps?

"Hey, Danny," Lemuel said with that condescending tone, ushering Louisa aside so that he could grin at him. "Made it to Upsilon yet? Is the boss finally letting you prove your worth, huh?"

Danford smiled as best he could—he knew that he was just teasing him. "No, not yet. Maybe someday."

Clara rubbed Danford's arm. "You'll have your chance, don't worry."

"Thanks," he said, but the misery left in Freja's wake was still tugging at his heart. It was hard for him to maintain his smile, so he looked away while the others bantered.

A few moments later, Greymore joined them with Epsilon Rowena.

"All right, listen up," Greymore called as he pulled the bar doors shut behind him. "I've received word from Andrew that wolves from the Brabus territory were seen crossing over into mine. It's your job to head out to the last place they were seen and patrol the area. Andrew saw only two of them, but I'm sending more of you just in case."

"What do we do if we see 'em, boss?" Lemuel asked.

"I'm trying to come to agreements with these packs, so if you can avoid a fight, it would be appreciated. If these wolves make a move, though, do what you gotta do," Greymore replied.

They all nodded and gave their words of understanding.

Greymore then looked at Danford. "Danny, if shit gets crazy, it's your job to get back here and tell me. Got it?"

Danford nodded, his heart thumping, "Y-yeah, I got it."

"All right, be safe, be careful, you know the drill," Greymore said. "Rowena, you're lead on this."

She nodded. "Got it, boss." Then, she moved through the small group and began leading the way.

Danford trailed behind the others. While he was relieved to have something to distract him from both Freja and the overbearing loneliness that gnawed at him, there was no shaking the fear curling inside his chest. He knew all too well what werewolves were capable of, especially when a territory dispute was at stake. Anything could happen out there, and the thought of fighting turned his stomach. He wasn't naïve enough to hope they'd encounter nothing—it never worked that way. He'd been with his pack long enough to know they were walking into something—whether it was a fight, a trap, or something worse.

The wolves around him were some of Greymore's best, seasoned and strong, but that didn't calm the anxiety buzzing beneath his skin. He felt like an outsider walking among them. They moved with confidence, while he struggled with his own unease.

Stepping off the ship and onto the icy docks, the chill bit through his coat, his breath visible in the cold air, but it wasn't the cold that bothered him. The streets of the Citadel were eerily empty, save for the soft glow of warm lights flickering from behind frosted windows. The smell of Yule foods—roasted meats, baked bread, spiced wine—filled the air, along with the sound of distant laughter and upbeat music from townhouses and privately booked bars. People were celebrating behind closed doors, lost in their warmth and joy.

It hurt more than he cared to admit. Seeing everyone inside, happy and surrounded by loved ones made his already aching heart throb harder. He walked the empty, frozen streets with packmates who, deep down, he knew saw him as a hindrance—a leftover, a charity case. He was there because Greymore felt sorry for him, not because he belonged.

That's what he told himself, anyway.

But a small part of him—one he tried so hard to bury—*did* mind. That part of him craved the sense of belonging that always seemed just out of reach, and the despair of not knowing where he truly fit only twisted the knife deeper. He wasn't sure he ever would find where he belonged. And at times like this, surrounded by the joy of others, that thought weighed heavier than ever.

He tried focusing on the mission, following his packmates to the edge of the city, and once they reached the tree line, everyone shifted into their wolf forms. But that was yet another thing that weighed down on him, making him feel out of place. Rowena was *huge*; not bigger than Greymore, but still huge. And so were the others; they had muscle, they had deadly talons and murderous bites, and they were as tall as men on all fours. But him? He was a runt, a scrawny, weak hindrance; every packmate had at least a foot of height on him. That was probably why his birth parents abandoned him.

Why was it all bothering him so much now? Before, he didn't care much—at least not this much. Was it because of Freja? Because she'd used and left him? Because he'd felt what he'd stupidly allowed himself to think was the pull of fate? Or was it because he'd been used twice in such a short space of time? Freja, Luther…. He didn't want to think about that disgusting man.

"Keep up, Danny," Rowena called.

Danford shook himself from his thoughts and hurried to catch up, falling into position within the patrol formation. The forest was eerily silent around them, the towering fir and spruce trees looming like dark sentinels under the heavy weight of snow. The sharp, crisp scent of pine filled the air, mingling with the icy cold that nipped at his fur. Their paws moved soundlessly over the thick blanket of snow, the only trace of their passage the occasional puff of breath hanging in the frozen air.

His senses were on high alert, every nerve tingling with anticipation as his eyes scanned the forest for any sign of movement. A flicker of shadow, the rustle of snow—anything that could betray the presence of hostile wolves. His heart pounded harder with each step, and though he tried to match the vacant, emotionless stare of the others, he could feel the tension pulling at him. His mind raced, unease twisting in his gut, and despite his best efforts to hide it, the anxiety gnawed at him, making it hard to keep up the calm façade.

And then Rowena stopped. The pack halted behind her, lowering their bodies into the snow, mirroring her every move.

Danford's heart thumped so hard against his chest that it felt like it might explode. He took deep but quiet breaths, trying to calm himself. But he caught half of the pack glancing back at him, and he knew what they were thinking. His silly little anxiety problem was going to get them caught, wasn't it?

"I've got a scent," came Rowena's voice. "Two wolves…no, three. Headed that way," she said, lifting her paw to point to her left.

"Snow's coming," Lemuel announced.

"Good," Clara replied. "It'll cover our tracks."

"And theirs," he retorted.

"There *are* no tracks," Rowena snapped. "Only scent. Noses up. Let's move."

They began moving again, keeping low to the ground, moving silently through the woods like snakes through the long grass. When they approached a towering oak tree, Danford finally locked on to the scent that Rowena had caught—it looked like *everyone* was finally catching it. If there was one thing he had going for him, it was his senses. They weren't as sharp as Rowena's—nobody's were, only Greymore—but they were sharper than every other wolf, even the Etas.

"Fuckers pissed up the tree," Lemuel snarled, approaching the trunk.

"Get back in formation," Rowena snapped at him.

He scoffed, glaring at the piss stain on the bark. "They're laughing in our fucking faces, Rowena. Look at this sh—"

A savage snarl snatched the silence away, and the sound of cracking foliage and Lemuel's yelp followed.

Danford shot up and darted for cover, his legs trembling as he watched it all happen. Three scruffy, scarred wolves burst out of the frosty brush, following the wolf who attacked Lemuel. At the same time, Rowena commanded the group to attack, and everyone but Danford burst into action.

He watched them clash, he watched the wolves snarl and snap and slash and bite. The hostile ones were bigger, brawnier, likely Epsilons or Betas, and they were relentless. But so were Dantord's packmates. While he hid behind a bush, just as he'd been trained, just as he'd been ordered, he observed the fight, waiting for Rowena to tell him to go for help.

But one of the hostiles broke away from Edward and Clara; it went for Rowena, who was already fighting the largest wolf alone, and there was no time for Danford to warn her. The beast collided with her, and within a matter of moments, just a few slashes and slices, she was down on the snow, bleeding, yelping, trying to fight them off.

Danford made the call himself. He stuck to the cover of the brush, moving as fast as he could; one good thing about his size was that it made him more agile, it made him quicker. The second he was clear of the battle, he raced through the woods as fast as his legs would carry him, leaping over the rocks, swerving past the fallen trees. Nobody was on the streets when he reached the Citadel, so he remained in his wolf form, running, heading for the docks. He sprinted up the steps, down below deck, and morphed into his human form and came to a skidding halt once he reached the bar.

Everyone was still partying, laughing and fumbling about. Danford huffed and puffed, his heart racing as he stumbled through the crowd, searching for Greymore. He found him by the bar, hollering and chortling while his inner circle of Betas and Epsilons told him jokes, trying to climb higher up the ladder than they already were, trying to impress their boss.

As much as he hated to do it, Danford interrupted, "G-Greymore." He took a deep breath, steadying his trembling legs as Greymore set his eyes on him. "I-it's Rowena—there's four of them, b-but they're *huge*. We need—"

"Ansel, Eldora, with me," Greymore said, losing his amused smirk and adorning his serious, determined glare.

Betas Ansel and Eldora followed as Greymore led the way to the door, and Danford stumbled after them. They raced up to the deck and down onto the docks, and once they were clear of noisy streets, they adorned their wolf forms and hurried towards the woods. Greymore didn't ask Danford for directions; he'd obviously already caught their trail. And within what felt like moments, they reached the brawl.

But Rowena wasn't moving. She lay still in the bloody snow, gaping wounds all over her body. Danford knew that she was dead, and the sadness that he'd been trying to escape returned as Greymore and his Betas rushed past him to join the fight. He knew it wasn't his fault; he'd done his job...but knowing that she was dead hurt. She was his packmate.

He took cover behind the same bush, watching as Greymore, in his *massive* wolf form, smacked one hostile away like a ragdoll; the wolf hit the oak tree, and its body cracked and snapped like a cheap toy. It fell and lay lifeless. And then the Alpha stormed over to the corpse and tore its head off with one effortless pull. He did the same to Rowena—he had to, didn't he? Lycans left dead too long in this world turned into hellhounds, and that was the last thing they needed.

With Greymore's help, Danford's packmates took the hostiles down in a matter of minutes, and once they were dead, everyone sat or laid down, panting, resting.

"Who were they?" Althea breathed, looking around at the headless corpses.

"They look like Hemlock Hollow wolves, boss," Ansel said, investigating one of the bodies. "Betas."

"Yeah, they have the hemlock pack mark," Edward said, looking at one of the others.

Greymore huffed and snarled. "These are the fuckers who've been ignoring our messages. Killed an izuret."

"Assholes," Lemuel grunted.

"Rowena," Solomon cried, nuzzling the Epsilon's lifeless body.

With a sympathetic sigh, Greymore went over to Solomon and patted his back. "I'm sorry, Sol. We'll bury her on our land, and we'll make sure she didn't die in vain."

Solomon looked up at him, scowling in despair. "We should hunt them," he growled, tears in his eyes. "All of them."

"All in good time. They killed in our territory, so we have every right to take the fight to them," Greymore replied sternly.

Danford felt sick. A pack war? He didn't want to fight, he didn't want to see everyone battling for their lives again. They'd barely made it out of Eltaria. A pack war might not be as widespread as the war back home, but it was a fight nonetheless, and just thinking about it made him want to throw up. How many more were they going to lose? First Rowena, and then…who? Anyone could die.

He wanted to try and steer Greymore away from the idea of starting a war, but Rowena had just died; he wasn't going to be the guy who made her death seem like it meant nothing.

"Let's move," Greymore called and picked up Rowena in his massive arms. "We get back to the ship, and we call a pack meeting. Looks like the celebrations are over." He then started leading the way back.

Although Danford was glad that they weren't rushing into a fight right this very second, he felt bad about Rowena—he felt bad for Solomon. His mate was dead, and Danford was certain that the pain of the loneliness that came with that tragic loss was a million times worse than the pain that *his* loneliness gave him. He considered giving Solomon his condolences, but he felt like it was too soon. He'd say something later. For now, he wanted to keep his senses peeled and focus on getting back to the safety of the Citadel.

Chapter Six

>—)) ☾ ((—<

Preparing for Retaliation

Yule celebrations were put on hold when Greymore and the scouting party returned. Everyone gathered in the bar, and Greymore told them what happened in the woods. The majority of the pack demanded their right for retaliation, and their leader didn't deny their request, he just had to tell Zalith first.

Danford then heard Freja's name and his heart started racing.

"Anyone know where she is?" Greymore asked, looking around the room, but his eyes settled on Danford for a moment.

He tensed up as his nervousness returned like a punch to his gut. As he looked away, he tried to calm down; if he didn't act normal, he'd look even guiltier. And he had no idea where she was.

Greymore sighed deeply. "All right. Randy, go to the grove and see if she's there. If she is, tell her the situation and bring her here. Nelson, go with him for safety."

Randy and Nelson nodded. They got up and left the bar.

"Althea, take Edward, Clara, and Lemuel. Go with Solomon to the woodland just behind where the compound is being built and bury Rowena. The rest of us will have time to grieve once we deal with the Hemlocks."

With their verbal confirmations, the instructed people picked up the makeshift coffin that they'd put Rowena in and left the bar.

Danford watched Solomon leave. He wanted to say something, but it still felt too soon. Maybe he'd send him flowers or something tomorrow.

"Everyone else, just…settle down and make sure you're ready for a fight," Greymore then said.

As Greymore left the room, conflicted murmurs echoed around the room, and Danford listened in. While some of his packmates were rearing to go, ready to avenge their fallen comrade, others had the same worries as he did. They'd escaped Eltaria to avoid dying in the war, and now they were getting themselves into another fight.

Danford rested his arms on the table and sighed deeply. He couldn't help but reminisce about the days when he was on his own and didn't have to deal with pack politics because he just kept at his own pace. Now, though, there were so many rules, ranks, and expectations. And a part of him wondered for a moment whether he should leave and go it as a rogue again. But that was stupid, wasn't it? He might not be the greatest member of the pack, but he *did* have it good here. He was just moping again, wasn't he? Why was he so…depressed?

With a shake of his head, he rested his head on his arms and waited.

And waited.

And waited.

And when he realized that the drawing he'd started working on was turning out to look like Freja, he scoffed embarrassedly and tucked the paper under another before putting his pen away.

Almost an hour passed until someone finally walked back into the bar, and when Danford saw that it was Randy and Nelson, he tensed up. He could smell Freja, he could *feel* her approach, and when she stepped through the door, he felt like his racing heart might explode as anxiety ensnared him. A part of him hoped she might glance his way, but she didn't look his way; she followed behind his packmates as if he wasn't there at all. And her three sisters followed, all with the same vacant expression as Freja.

But one of them…one of them shot him a glance, and her emotionless eyes widened ever so slightly, almost as if she'd noticed something.

Had Freja told her sisters about last night? It seemed that way, and it looked like her sisters hated him. Freja was never going to talk to him again, was she? His racing heart ached, like someone had driven a stake through it.

He helplessly watched as Freja and her sisters started talking with the Betas and Gamma. Freja still didn't spare him a glance, but he couldn't take his eyes off her. He gazed at her as she spoke, captivated by her golden hair, her amber eyes. It was hard to right off the urge to go over there, but he wouldn't embarrass himself or her like that. He'd stay where he was and keep trying to bury the dismay.

Greymore returned not long later with the wolves he'd sent to bury Rowena.

Danford sat up straight, watching as everyone took their seats or stood around the bar, watching Greymore, waiting for him to speak. This was it, wasn't it? It was time to talk battle, time to talk strategy, and time to assign people their roles. Danford knew that he'd likely be the one who ran for backup again, but he was fine with that. He was fast, after all.

"All right, listen up," Greymore called.

The room went silent.

"The Hemlock Hollow Pack crossed into our territory and killed one of us. We're executing our right to retaliate with Zalith's blessing. As far as we know, the Hemlocks have thirty-seven members: an Alpha and a Luna, three Betas—not including the ones we killed out there—a Gamma, six Epsilons, ten Enforcers, eight Etas, a Theta, two Iotas, a Kappa, two Lambdas, and one Omega." Greymore paused and leaned his back against the bar. "There are fifty-three of us, but most of the Hemlocks are well-trained and jacked as fuck, so it's gonna be two or three against one with some of 'em."

"How many?" Freja asked.

Her voice sent a shiver down Danford's spine; he thought he'd never hear it again. He just wished that she was speaking to *him*.

"I'm thinking two against each Beta, and three against the Gamma," Greymore answered. "You and I can take the Alpha and Luna."

Freja nodded. "My sisters can help with the Epsilons. Not Sophronia, though. We're not risking the baby," she said, glancing at her pregnant sister.

Greymore grunted in agreement. "Llewellyn can stay back with her."

"Are you sure?" Llewellyn, the dark-skinned, green-eyed man holding Sophronia's hand asked. "Won't you need me?"

"Protect your mate," Greymore said. "We've got enough fighters."

Llewellyn nodded appreciatively.

The Alpha's gaze then shifted to Danford. "Danny, you're on messenger duty, as per," he instructed.

Danford nodded. "Y-yeah, okay." He hoped that the mention of his name or his voice might grab Freja's attention, but she still didn't look his way.

"Freja, you'll lead team A, and I'll lead team B," Greymore continued. "There are two main ways into and out of the hollow, so we'll both enter from either or. That way, no one escapes."

"And we're just going for the kill?" Freja asked.

Greymore sighed deeply. "They've ignored our messages and killed an izuret; I think it's pretty damn clear that they're not interested in an alliance, especially after what happened this morning. But I'm going to give them one more chance to listen—"

"They killed Rowena!" Solomon cried out. "They deserve to—"

"And we killed the wolves responsible for her death," Greymore interjected firmly. "However, it *is* still our right to execute as many of them as we see fit. For all we know, though, there could be wolves in that pack who don't agree with their Alphas' choices. I want to give *those* wolves a chance to come forward."

Solomon looked utterly distraught, but everyone else seemed to understand.

Danford understood. The Alphas always had the final say; the voices of the lesser wolves, like Omegas and Upsilons, didn't matter. There *could* be members of the Hemlock Hollow Pack who didn't want war, and Danford had always appreciated Greymore's willingness to hear out *every* member, not just those with the loudest voices or the biggest muscles.

As Greymore went on to discuss formations and battle plans, though, Danford's eyes once again drifted to Freja. He gazed, hoping she might glance or turn her head, but her sights remained firmly fixed on Greymore.

Someone glanced at him though.

Sophronia.

When their stares locked, Freja's pregnant sister *glared* at him. The hostility in her golden eyes was thick and intimidating, and Danford meekly turned his head to look the other way.

"Tonight, an hour after sundown," Greymore's voice cut through the tense air.

Danford sharply shifted his gaze to him as the pack called their confirmations. *Tonight*? That was so soon. But he knew that these kinds of things were better dealt with sooner rather than later. What he *didn't* know was what team he was on; he'd been too busy staring at Freja and avoiding her sister's piercing gaze.

But he wasn't going to have to ask.

"You better not fuck up," Lemuel muttered as he passed Danford's table.

He knew that Lemuel was on team A...*Freja's* team. That made him more nervous than he'd probably been since he first talked with the Luna. They were going to war, and he was going to be part of her group. He'd be answering to her. She'd be relying on him. What if he fucked up? Well...it wouldn't matter, really...would it? Freja clearly wanted nothing to do with him; she wouldn't even spare him a glance. In fact, he was surprised that she hadn't suggested Greymore take him on his team instead. Or her sisters.

With a quiet sigh, he turned his back on the room and rested his head in his hands. He wasn't ready—he'd probably never be ready for another war so soon, pack or world. But he didn't have a choice. He had a job to do, and despite his overbearing emotions, he'd do his best to perform as Greymore expected.

Freja approached—he felt her aura, he inhaled her intoxicating scent. His heart raced, but when he looked over his shoulder, he watched her leave the bar with her sisters and Greymore. Once more, not a glance, not a single acknowledgement of his presence.

The dismay entangled his aching heart *again*, but he didn't know what he was expecting. He wasn't shocked. But he was still reeling, he was still drowning. Why couldn't he just...get over it? Every other time this had happened, he'd been over it by noon, but hours later, he remained trapped by the sadness that came with her leaving, the despair inflicted by her avoidance and complete dismissal of his existence. And the fact that her sisters were shooting him nasty looks didn't help.

He knew that he should stay away, that he shouldn't attempt to talk to her. Not only did he want to spare them both the embarrassment, but he was also certain that her sisters would attack him for getting too close. He wasn't going to risk that. He'd just have to keep trying to get over it. But how could he? He couldn't even distract himself because his drawings turned out looking like Freja, and despite the imminent battle, he couldn't think about all the dangers and risks, all he could think about was *her*.

"Solomon, wait," came Althea's concerned voice.

"Don't do it, man," Nelson called.

Danford looked over his shoulder—

Solomon ripped him out of his seat as if he were nothing but a doll and pinned him against the wall with a thud. "This is all your fault!" he shouted in his face as Danford grunted and panicked. "You useless, stupid fucking runt!"

"Put him down!" Clara insisted as she and everyone else hurried over.

"I-I did what I was supposed to do!" Danford insisted.

"You could've been faster!" Solomon yelled. "But you were too fucking slow!"

"Dude, stop," Randy said as he and Clara tried pulling him off.

But Solomon shoved them both away with his free arm. "He could've helped!" he cried, tightening his grip on Danford's throat.

Danford choked and closed his eyes as he slowly suffocated. "I-I did what Greymore said!"

"Put him down!" Clara growled and yanked Solomon away with a little more force.

As he hit the floor with a thump, Danford grunted and held his throat with both hands, choking, gasping for air.

Solomon tried fighting Clara off, but Nelson and Randy grabbed him, too—and Lemuel, although he looked reluctant, also stepped in.

Danford took his chance to shuffle away unseen and darted out of the bar. His breathing turned from gasps to despondent huffs as he hurried through the corridors and up onto the deck. What happened to Rowena *wasn't* his fault; he did his job, he went for help. There wasn't anything more he could have done.

He scowled despondently and sat by the stairs—there wasn't anywhere else he could go; every bar, restaurant, and tavern was closed to the public for Yule.

Maybe should find somewhere else to stay…just until things cooled down. Or maybe forever. What did he have to lose? But he couldn't leave yet. He wouldn't leave Greymore in the lurch; that man had done so much for him. He had to stay on the ship and wait until it was time to head to the hollow. After *that* was over, though…perhaps he'd find a hotel or bed and breakfast. Or a house. He had more than enough money.

Going his own way again was starting to feel more and more tempting every day, and this time…he might just do it.

Chapter Seven

>—) 🍎 (—«

Hemlock Hollow

D anford didn't see Freja for the rest of the afternoon. Greymore returned to the ship a few hours before sunset, but neither the Luna nor her sisters were with him. Danford couldn't help but wonder where she was, and his anxiety and embarrassment kept him from daring to ask, especially after this morning. Greymore had smelled her on him, and he didn't want to make his Alpha suspicious—well, any more suspicious than he already was.

He remained on the deck, and he was lucky enough to have been offered a cigarette by one of the crew currently on the holiday ghost shift. He made it last as long as he could, savouring it; he probably wouldn't see another for days since it seemed like all the stores were closed for Yule and the new year. Each drag relieved him just enough to stop his nervous, angst-enthralled heart from racing, and he considered scouring the streets for an open store so he could buy a pack, but there wouldn't be time for that. Everyone was slowly emerging from below, gathering on the deck.

Once the crowd grew larger, Danford stood up and lingered by the steps. Of course, his eyes searched for Freja, but they instead found Clara, who was heading over to him.

"Hey, Danny," she said softly, placing her hand on his shoulder. "Are you okay? I'm so sorry about Solomon. He just…needs to put the grief somewhere, you know?"

With a deep sigh, Danford flicked his cigarette butt over the ship and nodded. "Yeah, I get it. Don't worry."

Clara glanced over her shoulder at Solomon, whose eyes were red from crying. "He's calmed down a little now, but Greymore's put him on his team instead of Freja's."

Danford took his chance. "Where…where *is* Freja?"

"She's waiting just past the tree line. We're heading out to meet up with her soon." He nodded. "Okay."

"Are you all right? After earlier, we'd understand if you wanted to stay—"

"N-no, I'm good," he interjected. He didn't want to seem so weak as to stay behind after a little brawl. "I'm okay," he assured her.

"Okay," she said, smiling a little. "I've got to join my group, but if you need anything, let me know, okay?"

"Y-yeah, thanks."

Clara then disappeared into the crowd.

A heavy sigh escaped Danford's breath, but there was no time for overthinking.

"Let's move!" came Greymore's firm order.

One by one, the pack walked down the steps and followed Greymore through the shipyard. Danford stuck close to the back—as usual—and as they trailed the dark, icy streets, he once again found himself glancing into the windows of pubs and townhouses. He wondered if he might experience something like that someday...a family sitting around a Yule tree, eating a meal together, laughing and dancing around.

They neared the woods.

Danford stopped dreaming and focused, staring at the trees. And there it was *again*...Freja's intoxicating, ginger-like scent, and the golden shimmer of her hair in the moonlight. Her aura...her alluring, *consuming* aura. It was like a beacon calling to him, urging him nearer, *pleading* that he ran to it. His wolf begged, too. It clawed under his skin, writhing and whining, eager to get as close to Freja as it could.

"Get ready. Group up," came Greymore's voice.

Snapping out of it, Danford merged into the crowd of shifting wolves heading towards where Freja was waiting. But despite his attempts to hide, the Luna's two sisters watched him like hawks—starved, stalking hawks. They watched his every move, their golden eyes like spotlights, keeping a vicious glare on him.

He stopped behind his taller packmates and shifted into his wolf form, hoping to avoid the glares. Greymore repeated the plan, ensuring that everyone was confident, and then when he and his group headed west, Danford followed Freja's group to the east.

He'd probably never feel completely ready for a battle, but he'd do his best to grasp onto some sort of composure. The nervousness was eating away at him, even more so with Freja twenty feet ahead of him. His heart was thumping, and his deep, quiet breaths didn't help him calm down. At least he wouldn't have to fight, though; all he had to do was hide and wait to be told whether he had to go and get backup—this time, though, backup would be Zalith. Danford wasn't worried, though. He was fast. He'd make it to Cypress Estate in no time.

They reached the Brabus territory line just as the moons began their slow ascent over the jagged mountains, casting an eerie kaleidoscopic glow across the landscape. The moment they crossed, a cold, creeping sensation slithered down Danford's spine, his fur prickling as the weight of enemy territory pressed down on him. The silence felt different here—thicker, more oppressive, as if the very air held its breath, waiting for something to go wrong.

Every step felt heavy, deliberate, as the wolves moved cautiously, their senses on high alert. Danford's ears twitched, straining to catch even the faintest sound—the crack of a twig, the rustle of leaves—anything that might signal Etas patrolling nearby. His heart pounded, the stillness amplifying every breath, every whisper of movement. The trees loomed above them like silent sentinels, their twisted branches casting long shadows that seemed to stretch and shift with the moonlight.

Suddenly, a blur of motion. A fox shot out from the underbrush, its red fur a fleeting flash in the dim light. Every wolf froze in place, muscles tensed, teeth bared, ready for the fight they were sure was coming. Danford's breath caught in his throat, his body coiled like a spring—but then a collective exhale of relief came as they watched the small creature dart into the shadows and disappear.

Still, the unease lingered, hanging heavy in the air. They had crossed the line, and there was no telling what lay ahead.

Everyone came to an abrupt halt, sinking silently into the snow, their bodies blending with the pale, frozen landscape. Danford mimicked their movements, his heart pounding as his eyes darted around, searching for the unseen threat. His pulse quickened when he finally spotted it—an Eta, black and brown fur rippling in the moonlight, perched atop a large boulder. The wolf's gaze was fixed on the tree line, cautious and alert, but unaware of the danger creeping toward him. They were getting close to the hollow.

Danford's breath caught as Freja's sisters, their movements fluid and predatory, slipped through the snow like shadows, their bodies low and silent. The tension in the air was palpable, every second stretched thin as they inched closer to the unsuspecting guard. He barely dared to blink, his heart racing with anticipation.

In a matter of seconds, they struck—swift and deadly. The Eta didn't even have time to react before they were on him, their paws wrapping around him like iron grips. There was no sound, no struggle, just the cold efficiency of wolves trained for this very moment. The guard's body went limp, and they dragged him into the snow as his form shifted back to human, his unconscious body vanishing beneath the white blanket.

Danford let out a quiet breath, but the unease in his chest remained. The threat may have been neutralized, but with every step deeper into enemy territory, the danger felt closer, more real. As Freja's sisters rejoined the group, their eyes gleamed with the thrill of the hunt, and Danford knew it was only a matter of time before the real fight began.

The group pressed on, following Freja as she moved with quiet confidence, leading them deeper into enemy territory. Danford couldn't help but admire her, his eyes constantly drawn to the golden sheen of her fur as it caught the moonlight. Every time he looked at her, something in him stirred—an uncontrollable rush of emotions that he fought to suppress. He couldn't afford to be distracted, not now. He needed to be alert, ready for anything. But how could he focus when all he could think about was someone who barely acknowledged him? Someone he couldn't have, no matter how much his heart ached for it.

Shaking the thoughts away, Danford forced his attention back to their surroundings. The air grew colder, more biting as they delved deeper into Brabus territory, the familiar safety of their land now far behind. Every step they took felt heavier, the looming threat of what lay ahead gnawing at him. His ears twitched as another Eta came into view, this one standing watch atop a pile of logs, its eyes scanning the darkness.

Freja's sisters moved like shadows again, quick and lethal. Within moments, the guard was taken down as effortlessly as the first, his body disappearing into the snow, leaving no trace of their passage. Danford's pulse raced, the tension building in his chest as they continued their silent advance.

When they reached the top of the steep, shrub-covered hill, the group halted, gazing down into the hollow below—the heart of Brabus territory. The enemy pack's den lay sprawled in the valley, dimly lit by the cold glow of the moons. The air around them seemed to thicken with tension, the kind that came just before a storm broke. Danford's heart pounded in his chest, every muscle in his body tight with unease. They stood on the brink of something inevitable—*a fight*. The hollow was waiting, and there was no turning back now.

"Positions," Freja ordered.

Although her voice sent an anticipating sensation through him, Danford did as he was told. When his packmates moved to take their places, he headed down the side of the hill, using the snow and shrubs for cover. He followed Kira, the Eta who'd been told to stick close to him until he reached his spot—a towering boulder just behind the tree line. Kira then left him alone, and Danford did his very best to remain as calm as he could.

He waited…not daring to peer past the rock at the hollow. The sound of shuffling paws and snarling maws accompanied the howling wind; he hoped it wouldn't shift direction and carry his scent towards the hostiles.

But then he heard the commotion. Stomping paws, hostile snarls…and Greymore's voice.

Danford ever so slowly crept forward until he could see around the boulder. He watched Greymore emerge from the tree line and into the hollow, where the Hemlock Alpha waited with his pack behind him.

"You killed one of ours," Greymore growled.

The Hemlock Alpha chuckled cruelly. "I knew you'd come," he said, looking Greymore up and down. "The wolf who mingles with demons and vampires. The wolf from another world. An abomination."

Greymore snarled in hostility.

"Have you come to offer us allegiance? After *so many* failed attempts," he taunted.

"I've come to offer a chance to any wolf who doesn't want to die tonight," Greymore answered coldly.

Snarls and growls echoed through the hollow.

The Hemlock Alpha laughed loudly. "You dare threaten us? Those other weak, pathetic little dog packs might have fallen for your empty promises, but not us. Not me. You just...show up here and start taking over, taking land, turning packs, all while bowing to some filthy demon?" he snarled sourly. "Brabus, Citadel, Cypress Forest— it's *all* mine, and if I have to kill everyone you've turned against me, if they won't kneel as they should, their blood will be on your paws!"

His words made Danford feel sick. He really didn't want a fight to break out, but he knew that it was inevitable. Wolves were going to die tonight.

With a huff and a snarl, Greymore summoned his pack. Everyone emerged from the tree line, and the Hemlock wolves seemed to almost quiver at just how many of them there were. But their Alpha didn't back down. One smaller, beige-furred wolf did speak, and it sounded like she was trying to tell Greymore that she didn't want to fight, but the massive grey wolf beside her thwacked her head with his paw, silencing her.

"Get the fuck out of here while you can still walk," the Hemlock Alpha threatened.

Greymore chuckled darkly. "All right," the Alpha growled before lunging forward, grabbing the Hemlock Alpha with his massive hand-like paws. The tension broke, and the pack burst into action, wolves colliding in a frenzy of snarls and flashing teeth. Danford's muscles tensed, every instinct screaming at him to join the fight and protect *Freja*, but his orders were clear: hold position and wait. Wait until he was needed.

From his hiding spot, he had a perfect view of the chaos. The two packs clashed with ferocity, wolves crashing into each other with bone-crushing force. The sound of growls, howls, and the sickening rip of flesh filled the air. Danford watched in wide-eyed horror as the snow turned crimson, blood splattering across the battlefield. Wolves tore into one another with savage fury, teeth sinking into throats, claws raking across fur and flesh.

He could barely breathe, his throat tightening as he watched the carnage unfold. Bodies writhed in the snow, some in human form, others still shifting as they fought for their lives. The air was thick with the scent of blood, wet fur, and death. Danford gripped the snow beneath him with trembling paws, trying to focus, to be ready if the call for backup came. But all he could do was watch, helpless, as wolves he knew fought and bled before his eyes.

A Hemlock wolf—massive and snarling—was ripped apart by Greymore's second-in-command, its throat torn open in a spray of blood. The sight of it made Danford's stomach churn, but he forced himself to stay still, his breath coming in shallow, shaky gasps. He had to stay ready. He had to be prepared. But the madness playing out in front of him made it impossible to focus on anything other than the brutal reality of the battle.

Everywhere he looked, there was violence. A wolf shrieked as its hind leg was ripped clean off, blood spraying in an arc as it collapsed into the snow, shifting back into human form before it even hit the ground. Another, fur streaked with blood, had its jaw torn open by a vicious bite, collapsing into the growing sea of bodies.

Danford's pulse hammered in his ears, drowning out the sounds of the fight for a moment, but he forced himself to stay aware. He had to keep watching, waiting for the signal. But as the battle raged on, the sheer brutality of it all made his mind reel. He could feel his body tense and tremble, the adrenaline surging through him, but he stayed crouched, hidden behind the boulder.

Greymore and the Hemlock Alpha clashed again, their massive forms crashing into the trees, sending bark splintering into the air. The earth seemed to shake beneath the weight of their blows, the sound of snarling and snapping jaws echoing through the forest. Danford watched as they struggled for dominance, his heart pounding so hard it felt like it might burst from his chest.

Teeth flashed in the moonlight, claws raking through fur and flesh. A Hemlock wolf took a massive swipe to the throat, its life draining in seconds as it crumpled into the snow, shifting back to human form as it fell. Another wolf, fur matted and torn, dragged its teeth down the spine of a packmate, ripping flesh as it went. The sound of tearing skin and bone cracking was everywhere, punctuated by the deafening howls of pain and fury.

Danford wanted to fight, to help, but all he could do was wait. Wait in the cold silence of his hiding spot, watching the battle unfold, knowing that the call for backup could come at any moment—or not at all.

His eyes found Freja, and as he watched her fight, a conflicting mix of awe and fear swirled around inside him. She was handling herself, taking out the enemy, assisting packmates. But she'd taken a few blows; her golden fur was stained red, and the urge to run to her was stronger than Danford's urge to remain where he'd been told.

She didn't need his help, though.

Freja wasn't the one howling and crying in terror in the middle of the battlefield.

That small, beige-furred wolf who'd tried to speak up before the battle—there she was, huddled up between the sprawled, mangled bodies, shivering, whimpering, holding her paws over her head. No one was running to help her. No one saw her. No one cared.

Danford had been that wolf. He knew the terror that must be surging through her. He knew what it was like to be abandoned.

He was fast, and he was agile—probably the swiftest wolf there. He could get to her. He could save her. He was her only chance.

Terrified but determined, he darted out of his cover. He feared the repercussions of disobeying Greymore's order, but he'd take his punishment gladly knowing that he'd saved a life. A life that didn't seem to matter to anyone.

It mattered to *him*.

He scurried through the battle, dodging past bodies, heads rolling free from necks, limbs ripped clean off. His breath caught in his throat as he narrowly avoided a Hemlock wolf that lunged at him, its jaws snapping viciously inches from his face. The ground was slick with blood, the scent overwhelming; corpses littered the battlefield, some twitching with their last breath, others already gone. It was a massacre, a bloodbath all too familiar, and all around him, wolves continued to clash, to bite, to tear.

When Danford reached the terrified beige wolf, his heart sank. She lay frozen amid the chaos, her wide, tear-filled eyes staring blankly at the carnage around her. He nudged her with his muzzle, urging her to her paws, but she remained still, trembling, her entire body locked in fear. Words were useless—they weren't of the same pack, and neither of them were Alphas, so they couldn't communicate beyond the instincts shared by wolves. But that didn't stop him from trying. He couldn't just leave her there.

"Come on!" he insisted, his voice filled with urgency as he pressed his muzzle against her side, lifting her slightly. She stared at him in horror, her eyes glistening with tears that streaked down her fur. But something in his desperate action seemed to break through the haze that held her captive. Slowly, shakily, she began to move.

Danford turned and ran, his paws barely making contact with the blood-soaked snow. He could hear the sounds of battle crashing behind him—snarls, the wet crunch of teeth sinking into flesh, the cries of wolves in pain—but he kept his focus on the path ahead. The beige wolf followed him, slower than him, but she kept close, her breath coming in ragged gasps.

They weaved through the battlefield, dodging bodies and the spray of blood that filled the air. Danford's ears rang with the sounds of death, the brutality unfolding around them, but he couldn't afford to look back. He couldn't risk losing focus now. His only goal was to get her to safety, back behind the boulder that had been his refuge only moments before.

But the chaos was unrelenting. A massive grey wolf lunged out of nowhere, its jaws snapping dangerously close to the beige wolf's hind leg. Danford skidded to a halt, fear gripping him for a split second before he instinctively lashed out, baring his teeth and snarling at the attacker. The grey wolf hesitated, but only for a heartbeat before another member of Greymore's pack tackled it to the ground.

"K-keep going!" Danford insisted, nudging the beige wolf forward again, urgency searing through him. Her pace quickened, but it was clear she was struggling. Every step she took was laboured, and Danford could sense the exhaustion weighing her down, threatening to pull her under. His own muscles burned with effort, but he couldn't stop. He wouldn't let her fall behind.

As they neared the boulder, the ground shook beneath them as a heavy crash echoed through the trees—Greymore and the Hemlock Alpha, still locked in their brutal struggle. The force of their battle sent shockwaves through the earth, making Danford stumble.

He recovered quickly, but the beige wolf faltered, her legs giving out from under her as she collapsed into the snow.

Panic surged through him. They were so close. "Get up!" Danford begged, circling back to her, his muzzle nudging her shoulder, trying to get her back on her feet. Her breath came in ragged gasps, her eyes filled with terror and exhaustion, but she managed to push herself up once more.

Danford led the final sprint to the boulder, every second feeling like an eternity. The battle raged around them, and Danford could feel the presence of wolves closing in, the chaos drawing nearer, but they made it. As they dove behind the boulder, Danford felt the cold stone press against his side, offering a brief moment of shelter from the madness.

Panting, he glanced at the beige wolf. She lay beside him, her sides heaving with effort, but she was safe—for now.

Danford's eyes locked onto the massive figures of Greymore and the Hemlock Alpha, their forms towering over the rest of the wolves ensnared in combat. The two leaders clashed again and again and again with a ferocity that sent rumbles through the ground, the sound of their bodies colliding like thunder in the frozen night sky.

Greymore moved with brutal efficiency, his powerful hand-like paws swiping through the air, claws flashing as they connected with the Hemlock Alpha's side. Blood sprayed across the snow, but the Hemlock Alpha didn't back down. He retaliated with a savage lunge, his jaws snapping shut around Greymore's shoulder, teeth sinking deep into flesh. Greymore snarled in pain, but he didn't falter—he twisted his body, wrenching himself free, blood dripping from the ragged wound.

Danford's heart raced, his chest tightening as the battle grew more vicious. Greymore was injured, but so was the Hemlock Alpha. Deep gashes marred the enemy's dark fur, and one of his eyes was swollen shut from a previous blow, yet he fought on with the same wild, unrelenting fury. The ground beneath them was slick with blood, the air thick with the scent of iron and violence.

The two wolves circled each other, eyes locked, each looking for an opening. Danford's paws dug into the snow, his whole body tense as he watched. He could see the wear on both of them—the heavy panting, the blood seeping from their wounds—but neither was ready to give in.

With a deafening snarl, the Hemlock Alpha lunged again, his jaws aimed for Greymore's throat. Danford's eyes widened in horror as he saw the killing blow coming—but Greymore was faster. He sidestepped just in time, using the Hemlock Alpha's momentum against him. With a powerful strike, Greymore raked his claws down the Alpha's side, tearing through fur and muscle, leaving deep, jagged wounds in his wake.

The Hemlock Alpha howled in pain, stumbling, but Greymore didn't let up. He pressed the attack, his movements a blur of fury and precision. He slashed again, this time catching the Alpha across the face, and blood spattered into the air as the enemy staggered backwards.

Danford's pulse raced, his eyes glued to the scene as Greymore roared with unbridled rage. The Hemlock Alpha was weakening, his once-powerful body now trembling with the effort to stay upright. Blood poured from his wounds, staining the snow around him a deep crimson, but he refused to fall. With a final snarl, he charged one last time, desperate, wild—but Greymore was ready.

In one swift, brutal movement, Greymore sidestepped the charge and slammed the full force of his massive paws into the back of the Hemlock Alpha's head, sending him crashing to the ground. The sound of bone hitting stone echoed through the battlefield as the Alpha lay stunned, dazed, and unable to rise.

Danford's heart pounded in his ears as he watched Greymore stand over the fallen Alpha, his breath heavy, his fur matted with blood. For a moment, the world seemed to fall still. The sounds of the battle around them faded as Greymore raised his claws, his eyes dark with determination.

And then, with a savage roar, he brought his claws down in a single, decisive strike. The Hemlock Alpha's head rolled free from his body, blood gushing from the severed neck. It was over. The lifeless body crumpled to the ground, and Greymore stood victorious, his massive frame looming over the fallen Alpha.

Danford stared in wide-eyed silence, the reality of the moment sinking in. The battle still raged around them, but the sight of the beheaded Hemlock Alpha sent a ripple of fear through the remaining wolves.

Greymore had won.

And across the battlefield, Danford found Freja again, her golden fur blazing like fire under the moons. She moved with a lethal grace through the frenzy, her eyes locked on her target—the Hemlock Luna. The air between them crackled with tension, the unspoken challenge hanging heavy.

The Hemlock Luna, a towering wolf with sleek, dark fur and eyes as cold as the winter night growled low in her throat. She stood at the centre of the carnage, powerful and unyielding. Her packmates fought and died around her, but her focus never wavered from Freja. This wasn't just a fight for territory—it was personal. The air between them seemed to thrum with years of hatred and rivalry.

Freja didn't hesitate. With a ferocious snarl, she lunged forward, her muscles rippling as she launched herself at the Luna. The Hemlock Luna met her halfway, their bodies crashing together in a blur of claws and teeth. The impact sent a shockwave through the battlefield, and for a moment, all Danford could hear was the deafening clash of their battle.

They rolled together across the blood-soaked snow, snapping and slashing at each other. Freja's golden fur was soon streaked with crimson as the Luna's claws raked down her side, but she fought through the pain, twisting her body and sinking her teeth into the Hemlock Luna's shoulder. The dark-furred wolf howled in pain but retaliated with a vicious swipe to Freja's face, sending her stumbling back.

Danford's breath caught in his throat as Freja staggered, blood dripping from a deep gash above her eye. But she didn't falter. With a snarl that sent shivers down his spine, she darted back into the fight, her movements quicker, sharper. The Luna snarled, swiping her paw at Freja again, but this time Freja was ready. She ducked low, narrowly avoiding the blow, and then launched herself upward, her teeth sinking into the Luna's throat.

The Hemlock Luna let out a strangled howl, thrashing wildly as Freja held on, her jaws locked tight. Danford watched, breathless, as the Luna fought to shake her off, her claws slashing wildly at Freja's sides. But Freja's grip was relentless, her golden fur soaked in blood—some hers, some the Luna's. With a final, powerful shake, she threw the Luna to the ground, pinning her with a savage snarl. The Luna's eyes widened with the realization of her defeat, but there was no mercy in Freja's gaze. With one swift, brutal movement, Freja's claws slashed across the Luna's throat, the sound of tearing flesh cutting through the air.

The Luna's body went limp, her dark eyes glazing over as the life drained from her. Freja stood over her, panting heavily, her golden fur matted with blood, but victorious. Danford felt a surge of relief and awe as he watched her, his heart still racing from the tension of the battle. Freja then barred her teeth and savagely tore at the corpse's throat, removing the head before something far more deadly could possess the body.

Freja didn't linger over her kill. She lifted her head, her eyes blazing with the fire of the fight as she surveyed the battlefield. There was still work to be done, but the Hemlock Luna was dead, and Freja had proven once again that she was more than worthy of her place as the pack's Luna.

Danford swallowed hard, his chest swelling with a strange mixture of pride and something else, something deeper that he couldn't quite name. Freja was a force of nature, and watching her fight was both terrifying and enthralling.

The battle slowly died down as the Hemlock wolves realized that their Alphas were dead. Some tried to flee, but Danford's packmates made quick work of the cowards. Those who remained…well, they had only two choices: flee and die…or submit and join Greymore's pack.

Wolves began bowing their heads, and when he was sure that it was safe, Danford urged the beige wolf beside him to join the submitting survivors.

She understood. With a shaky exhale, she followed him out from behind the boulder, and when Greymore's scowling gaze hit them, she bowed her head, frozen.

Greymore dropped to all fours. He prowled through the bowing, resting crowd, heading towards Danford and the beige wolf.

Danford's heart raced, anxiety enthralling him. Was he about to be punished for leaving cover? Right here? *Right now*?

The Alpha stopped a few feet in front of them. His deep, dark eyes looked the beige wolf up and down for a few moments, but then his gaze shifted to Danford. "Danford," he said firmly, rising to his hind legs.

He obediently stared up at Greymore.

"I saw you save this wolf," he said, glancing at the beige wolf beside him. "And I think the majority of the pack would agree that your heroic…although disobedient act has earned you the right to become Upsilon."

Danford's racing heart skipped several beats, and his eyes widened. Had he just heard Greymore right? Upsilon? He gawped up at him, taking it in. "W-what?" He was happy—of course he was—but because he was raised human, there was a part of him that felt as if he could be happier, gladder. He still felt as if he didn't fit in, but…perhaps this was some sort of step in the direction he wanted to be going in.

"You're Upsilon," Greymore said, patting Danford's shoulder with his huge hand. "You've earned it. Time to figure out what you wanna do full-time." He then turned to face the battlefield. "The battle's over. You're all part of my pack now. Initiation will begin as soon as we're back. Let's move!"

And with that, it was over. The surviving Hemlock wolves followed the pack; Greymore's wolves kept a close eye on them all, but not one tried darting away.

The beige wolf ran beside Danford; he didn't yet know her name, but he'd make sure to get it after she was properly initiated into the pack. He was glad that he was able to save her—he was glad that he'd done something more useful than just hiding behind a rock and waiting to be sent to get backup. And now that he was Upsilon, he had a lot more to think about. He had to decide what his role would be, and there was a lot to choose from, a lot to consider. Not now, though. It was late, and all he wanted to do was rest and put the horrific sight of the battle behind him.

Chapter Eight

✦— ☽ 🜨 ☾ —✦

Peris

The kaleidoscopic moonlight and the glow of the orange lanterns lit the deck. Every wolf crowded the space, some having to take to the quarterdeck and forecastle deck to make room for the new recruits—no human was awake this late, and if they were, they weren't hanging around the shipyard; this night was the perfect cover for the initiation ceremony.

Danford usually stood alone, but the beige wolf he'd rescued clung to him like a magnet. Clara made sure to congratulate him on his promotion before joining her friends, and he caught the murmurs of Solomon, who didn't think he should have been named Upsilon.

Danford ignored the whispers, though. He glanced around the deck, watching as Greymore began accepting each wolf one by one into the pack. When it was the beige wolf's turn, she shyly approached Greymore, but it was over in a heartbeat; Greymore gave her the mark, and just like that, Danford heard her voice—

"I…I'm Peris," she said nervously, returning to his side.

He smiled awkwardly. "Uh…Danford."

Peris giggled as she wagged her tail excitedly. "I never thought anything like this would happen. We all thought we'd be trapped there forever." She lunged closer, hugging him as best she could in her wolf form. "Thank you for saving me, Danford."

Danford didn't immediately hug back; he felt a little startled. But when he did eventually move a paw around her, he caught Freja's stare. For the first time since she'd disappeared from his bed, she was looking his way, and he was struck with guilt. He didn't understand why he felt so guilty, but every instinct inside him told him to let go, to push Peris away. She wasn't the one he wanted to hold, she wasn't the one he wanted to be so close to.

And when he saw the *anger* gleaming in Freja's golden eyes, he tensed up and let go of Peris, stepping back as naturally as he could.

"Congrats on becoming Upsilon, though," Peris said, seemingly unbothered. "I'm still just an Omega, but maybe I'll actually have a chance of being seen here. Orson and Celeste were…well…not very nice would be an understatement."

"Well, most of the people are nice here, so I hope you'll be okay," he replied and glanced at Freja again, watching as she averted her gaze to her sisters. But there was something else lingering in her eyes, and the first thing Danford thought was: jealousy? But then the confusion hit him again. Was it actually jealousy, or was he just imagining it just like he'd convinced himself that he'd felt the pull of fate?

"Most?" Peris asked.

"Uhh…yeah, most," he said with an awkward laugh. "I think people just don't like me very much, though. I'm not as social as I think they'd like me to be."

"Oh…well, there's nothing wrong with wanting to be alone," she said with a frown. "Not everyone's a party guy, right?"

Her answer was a little refreshing; he didn't get that perspective from werewolves very often. "Exactly," he said in response.

Peris then looked around as the pack started disappearing below deck. "So…what do we do for fun around here? Are we allowed into the city? Orson and Celeste never let us go to the Citadel," she said as she moved closer to the edge and stared out at the icy, quiet city.

"Yeah, of course. We can do whatever we want as long as we come when we're called," he said but found his gaze drifting to Freja once again. He just…really liked her, and he didn't want her to be mad at him. He couldn't tell if she hated him in general or was mad at him because he was talking to Peris. If that were the case, though, wouldn't the Luna storm over and tell Peris to back off? The idea actually kind of delighted him; it would assure him that Freja was more than a one-night stand in both their eyes. But the Luna didn't leave her sisters' side.

With an excited smile, Peris leaned closer to him. "So…we can go now?"

Taking his eyes off Freja again, he stared at the beige wolf in startle. "Uh…we like you and me?"

She nodded. "You can show me around."

"Oh…" he drawled, once again glancing to where Freja was. He felt conflicted; he wanted to talk to the Luna, but everyone was around, so it wasn't a good idea, was it? He wished that there was some discreet way he could talk to her, but he had no idea what she'd even say because they weren't anything to each other, were they? He didn't want to be weird or offend her. However, he didn't want to tell Peris to go away, either; he wouldn't mind having a friend. So he said, "Okay. We uh…should probably shift out of our wolf forms, though."

That was when Peris adorned an embarrassed frown. "I didn't even think about that. I don't…have any clothes."

"There's a room full of spare clothes below deck. It's uh…this way," he said, unsure about letting Freja see him walk downstairs with Peris; it made him feel guilty and stupid. But again…it wasn't like he and Freja were anything to each other, right? He sighed and led the way, trying to shake the feeling of the Luna's watchful gaze following his every move. "Just over here," he said once they reached the bottom of the stairs. He nodded to the door to the right of the steps. "You go on in and get changed. I'll wait out here and go in when you're done."

With a nod, the beige wolf went into the room and pushed the door shut with her back leg. A few minutes went by, but she eventually re-emerged, and she wasn't what he'd imagined. She looked around his age, and her hair was a light blonde; it was a little bit of a mess, like she'd used her fingers to brush it. Her eyes were as green as summer grass, and a small scar sat on her left cheek. She'd chosen one of the white off-shoulder silk dresses and a red cardigan, along with a pair of red heels. She smiled brightly at him, stroking her dress.

He tried to hide any expression from his face, but he was certain that his eyes widened a little—she was *really* pretty. "Uh…is the dress okay?" he asked nervously.

Peris nodded, glancing down at it. "Does it suit me? I haven't worn a dress in so long."

"Y-yeah…it looks really pretty," he said, trying to hide that he felt awkward.

She then opened the door for him. "Your turn."

"Oh, I have my own clothes in my room," he said with a light chuckle.

"You have a room?" she asked, wide-eyed. "Will *I* get a room?"

"Probably, but…you'll likely be sharing with one or two others; there's a lot more of us now," he said, and the talk of rooms made him think about Luther. The only reason he now had his own private space was because of him, and he asked himself…could he keep that room without feeling disgusting?

"That's okay," Peris said. "I'd just…like a bed, you know? Sleeping on the forest floor, especially in the winter." She shook her head. "I haven't slept in a bed in…oh, it's been ten years already," she mumbled sullenly.

Danford frowned. "Were you…turned?"

She nodded and rolled up her left sleeve, revealing an old, scarred wolf bite. "It was Orson. He bit me and my brother, but…well, you know how it is. Alpha venom can kill humans, and Pete just…he wasn't as strong as me," she explained sadly, rolling her sleeve back down. She then flicked the scar on her face. "He cut my face when I tried to run, too."

Her words cut deep. They slapped his face, making him understand just how privileged he was despite the Eltarian war. Greymore's pack wasn't like the others out there; they'd always had clothes and food and each other. And Peris? She'd clearly been through her own type of hell.

He exhaled deeply and said, "Well, I hope you have an easier time here, and if you ever have any problems, you can bring them to Greymore; he's very big but very nice." He tried assuring her, and her smile convinced him that he'd succeeded.

"So...we just...call him Greymore? Not Alpha Greymore?"

"Uhhh..." he drawled, starting to head towards his room. He knew that the Aegisguardian werewolves had different customs; they all referred to their packmates as Alpha Greymore or Luna Freja or Eta whoever—title, name. Greymore didn't have a problem with either or, but he felt it was probably better that Peris stuck to Aegisguard's traditions. "Maybe stick with Alpha for now," he said with a small laugh.

"So...since I'm an Omega, I suppose I should be calling you Upsilon Danford," she said with a giggle.

He felt a little embarrassed about that. "N-no, no, you can just call me Danford— well, Danny, actually. People usually just call me Danny," he said, reaching his room.

She smiled and nodded. "Okay. Danny," she said and glanced at the door. "Is this your room?"

"Yeah," he said but hesitated. Freja's scent was still lingering in his room, and not only did he not want Peris to catch a hint and question him or make assumptions, but he also didn't want Peris' scent to mingle with and possibly overpower Freja's. "I'll uh...just be a minute or so."

Peris nodded. "Okay."

He slinked into his room and closed the door behind him with his back paw. But when he saw the same izuret from this morning sitting on the couch with a box of chocolates from his shelf, he frowned irritably. After shifting into his human form, he asked the creature, "What are you still doing here?"

With a squeak, it told him that it had nowhere else to be until the new year.

Danford rolled his eyes and went over to his dresser. "So, you're just gonna hang out in my room until then?"

It shrugged and went back to looking through one of Danford's sketchbooks, which it had on the seat beside it.

He took out some new clothes and pulled them on as he said, "Okay...well, clean up after yourself, please."

The creature squeaked its confirmation.

Once he slipped on some shoes and fitted his eyepatch, Danford left the room.

"O-oh," Peris gasped as he stepped out into the hall. "You're a lot cuter than I imagined," she said with a smile, looking him up and down.

He couldn't help but blush. "Oh...thank you," he said, dragging his hand over the back of his head.

"What happened to your eye?" she asked curiously.

"Gryphon attack," he said with a shrug.

Her eyes widened, filled with excitement. "You've seen gryphons?!" But then she frowned. "Oh, sorry."

"It's okay, don't worry," he said as he started leading the way through the corridor again. "But yeah, I've seen quite a few of them. They're actually pretty beautiful creatures when they're not attacking your face."

She giggled again. "I've only ever seen basilisks—those big...scaled, chicken things." Her smile faded into a frown. "One of them was nesting a mile from Orson's territory line. He took us all to kill it; we left the hollow as ninety, came back forty," she said with a sigh. "And he didn't even really seem to care how many we lost."

Danford shook his head. "He doesn't sound like he was a very good person."

"He wasn't, but...he was our Alpha. We had to keep these kinds of opinions to ourselves," she said as they climbed the stairs to the deck.

"I kinda hate that about being what we are—not that I'm super outspoken, but still."

"Is it like that here? Should we keep our opinions of the higher-ups to ourselves?"

"I would at least until you're comfortable and have gotten to know everyone."

"Okay, well—"

"Where do you think you're going?" Freja's voice interjected. Her question might seem like it was for the both of them, but...her gaze was fixed entirely on Danford, a clashing concoction of confusion, anger, and perhaps jealousy in her golden eyes.

Danford tensed up, his eyes widening as he stared at her. He thought she'd never talk to him again. "Uh...n-nowhere," he answered. "Peris just asked me to show her around the city."

Freja's gaze shifted to Peris, who was frozen. Her eyes filled with hostility, and she almost snarled at the girl. "You're meant to be with the others in the lounge," she snapped. "Go. Now!"

With a frantic nod, Peris turned around and scurried back downstairs.

Then, Freja set her eyes back on Danford.

"Is...everything okay?" he asked nervously.

She opened her mouth to speak—

"Freja," one of her sisters interrupted, appearing beside her. "What are you doing over here? With this...one-eyed Omega," she said condescendingly, looking Danford up and down as if he were an unsavoury meal.

"Opal, I told you to—"

"I'm not going to stand around and watch this *thing* play mind games with you. Come on. We need to get back to the grove."

"Mind games?" he questioned.

But Opal just shot him a hostile glare.

And so did Sophronia and Verity from across the deck.

Freja hesitated. She looked at Danford, and there was regret in her eyes, perhaps even a little sorrow. But she did as her sister asked; she turned around and walked away from Danford without another word.

Danford watched her leave, utterly confounded. She was acting like they were dating, but they weren't... and she listened to her sister when she was rude about him, so he didn't know what to think. He didn't want to hurt her feelings, but he also had no idea what was going on. And on top of that, he felt back for Peris; she just wanted to see the city. A part of him wanted to take her out anyway... but the last thing he wanted to do was piss Freja off and get people involved because he was being insubordinate.

With a huff and a sigh, he turned around and headed downstairs. Once he got to his room, he wrote a note,

Sorry we didn't get to go to the city, I don't know what that was about. We can probably hang out soon.

Danny.

and drew a rough picture of a gryphon before he handed it to the izuret. "Can you take this... and these—" he grabbed a trio of ribbon-wrapped peppermint candy canes, "—to Peris, please? She's the light blonde with the scar on her cheek. She's wearing a white dress and a red cardigan."

The izuret took the note and candy from him and saluted. Then, it flew out his window, leaving a collection of chocolate wrappers all over the couch.

He sighed and cleaned up after it, and once he was done, he poured himself a shot of whiskey, downed it, and fell into bed. It had been a long, draining, confusing, dismaying day... but at least he made a friend, right? At least he finally made it to Upsilon. But neither of those things outweighed the despair. It grew stronger the longer he lay there, and the emptiness in his heart grew wider, deeper. Freja had finally shown her face, she'd finally spoken to him, but it meant nothing—at least it felt like it didn't. He still felt that intoxicating longing for her, her wolf still pleaded that he got as close as he possibly could, but... why? For what? He didn't understand. It didn't make any sense. And as he lay there in the light of the single lit lantern, he wondered if he'd ever be free from the cage of despair and confusion that his and Freja's meeting had locked him inside.

Chapter Nine

>-) 🜚 (-<

An Unexpected Visit

Danford woke when he heard his door open. Assuming that it was the izuret leaving after earlier returning, he closed his eyes and tried to fall back asleep. But then someone or something a lot bigger climbed onto his bed, and he flinched and shot up—

"Sorry," came Freja's voice.

As his eyes adjusted to the dark, he watched Freja lay down beside him. Confusion struck him at the same time as her intoxicating scent, and he had no idea what to say or do. All he could think to ask was, "I-is everything okay?"

Freja rested her head on his pillow, gazing at him with her golden eyes. "Yeah, I just…" she paused and sighed. "I'm sorry for what Opal said earlier; she's just being protective—they're all like that."

"Protective of what? I didn't even do anything," he said with a nervous chuckle.

She shrugged. "I told them about last night—I needed someone to talk to. But it didn't exactly go as I thought it would, and now they're convinced that you're going to use me or something," she mumbled.

That upset him. He wasn't that type of person and knowing that they were likely judging him based on his rank made him feel worse. "Oh…" he said disappointedly.

"And I thought that maybe you becoming Upsilon today would change their opinions, but it's like… I don't know," she cut herself off and shook her head, sounding frustrated.

Why did she want them to change their minds? Did she… actually like him? "Oh…" he replied again. "Um.…" He didn't know what he wanted to say.

"I guess because they're all married to like Betas, they think that I should marry one, too—like actually marry or mate to or whatever. Verity thinks that I should just settle for Greymore," she grumbled.

Danford nodded. Although he understood why her sisters would think that, he hated it. But then it hit him, and his eyes widened. Was Freja…saying that she wanted to *marry him*? No…that was crazy. He was thinking too hard. "Greymore's cool," he said in response.

Freja sighed deeply and shook her head. "But he's not…*mine*," she said despondently. Anxiety and dismay filled her eyes as she gazed at him, and as an unsure frown appeared on her face, she looked away from him and asked, "So, what were you doing with that Peris girl?"

He shrugged and said, "Nothing. She said that she wasn't allowed to leave the forest for like ten years or something, and she really wanted to see the city, so I agreed to show her around."

"Hmph," Freja murmured.

A long silence dragged out between them.

It was getting *very* awkward *very* fast, so Danford desperately tried to think of something to say. All that came to mind, though, was something he'd wondered earlier. "Did you know Celeste? The Hemlock Luna."

Freja didn't immediately answer; she seemed hesitant. But after a few more silent moments, she huffed and said, "Yeah, a long time ago. Her full name was Celeste Nomery; her family owned the Nomery Farmstead in Dor-Sanguis. We met when my pack were travelling the country in search of better hunting grounds. It was just her and her parents, Alphas of a dead pack. We offered to take Celeste in. She hung around our camp for a while, but one morning, she was just gone, and so were all our valuables; she fled Dor-Sanguis just before the war got bad, left her parents behind. We lost track of her once she reached the coast."

That made him feel a little sick. "I could never leave my family like that."

"I guess she found her perfect match," she mumbled. "Orson was a nasty piece of work. A lot of stories travelled from pack to pack. Apparently, one winter, when things got really bad, he killed and fed Omegas to his pack. They all fucking ate their own like they were caribou."

His stomach turned. "W-what?" He was glad that they didn't do that here; he would have been eaten a long time ago if they did.

"Werewolves do some fucked up things sometimes."

Danford nodded. "I guess we're pretty lucky."

"What…happened to your parents?" she then asked.

He sighed despondently. "They lived very happy lives up until my mom got sick for a few years and eventually passed. Then my dad had a heart attack about a year later and didn't make it." He paused as his heart ached in his chest. "But I guess it might have been for the best because the war happened not very long after, and they were getting up there in age."

Freja slowly slid her palm down his arm and gripped his hand. "I'm sorry," she said sadly. "They sound like they were amazing people."

Danford's heart continued to ache, but it wasn't only with the sorrow of his parents' passing. No, it ached because he wanted to hug Freja. He wanted to hold her, to inhale her intoxicating scent, to become lost in her. But he was afraid of how she might react, and he was afraid that it might make it harder for him to ignore the overwhelming feelings brewing inside him.

He stared up at the ceiling, focusing on the gentle swaying of the ship. "They were," he replied. "I think it would have been a little easier if I had siblings to help share the grief with, but I made it through in the end," he murmured.

"Well, you're strong," Freja assured him. "You've made it through a lot, and now you're Upsilon. Do you know what role you want to pursue?"

Danford was surprised to hear someone call him strong, especially someone like Freja. *No one* had ever said that to him. "No," he chuckled. "I have no idea what good I can provide by being a higher rank."

"Well, you're fast and smart. If we lived out in the woods, I'd suggest Cupitor. But there's no need for runs into civilization. You could always train to be a Lambda or an Iota. I could see you as a hunter or a healer."

Her compliments made his heart flutter. "Well…Lambda would be fine, but would we still need to hunt if we're this close to civilization?"

She laughed a little. "You know Greymore. He's going to want to be out there catching deer and rabbits fresh from the forest instead of sending someone to buy something from the butcher."

He smiled and amusedly said, "That's true." And then he frowned curiously, glancing at her. "What would you do if you weren't so high ranked?"

Freja sighed and squeezed his hand—she was still holding it. "When I was a kid, my sisters and I used to love exploring the lesser-known parts of our territory. We'd map the place out, explore all the caves and the ravines. You know, the kinda stuff that Etas do when packs settle in new territories. So, I guess…I would have chosen to become an Eta—I think my sisters would have, too. But we were born Alphas, so we don't get to explore and make tunnels in the snow."

Danford was convinced that he'd feel the same way if he was in her position. "Sometimes…I hate being a werewolf," he muttered sadly.

"Yeah, me too," she said with a deep exhale. She kept hold of his hand but turned onto her side and leaned up onto her arm, looking down at him. "If you could choose, what would you rather be?"

"Hmm…" he pondered for a few moments, but nothing came to mind. "I'm not sure, actually. What about you?"

"Perhaps...förvandlare...like Mikael, the shapeshifter that came with you from Eltaria. That way, I could be whoever and whatever I want whenever I want. One day I could be an elf, the next, I could be...I don't know, a katokirinkata."

"Oh, that's a really good idea." He tensed up a little but fought through the nervousness as he reached up and tucked a few strands of her curly, golden hair behind her ear. "You'd look cute with little cat ears."

Freja giggled and stroked her fingers through Danford's hair. "So would you."

He blushed a little. "My first thought was vampire or demon, but they have the same set-up as werewolves in one way or another, so it probably wouldn't feel any better."

"And depending on who turns them, vampires can't walk in the sunlight. I couldn't imagine a life like that. I mean...if I was one who *could* walk in sunlight, then maybe it wouldn't be so bad. Their rules and stuff aren't as strict as demons and werewolves."

"Oh, yeah...that's true. I forgot about the sunlight thing," Danford said with a grimace. "If shapeshifter wasn't an option, I think I'd like to be a little forest animal or something that no one ever really bothers."

She smiled and said, "That *would* be nice. A peaceful little life."

"I could find a way to use my paws to draw all day."

Freja ran her fingers through his hair again. "Are you looking forward to the compound being finished?" she asked, changing the subject. "Our own little place, our own houses. More space. The smell of the forest." She sighed longingly as her eyes examined every inch of Danford's face. "We could just...run through the grass, find a little place to lay in the sun. Forget everything for a while."

Danford smiled at the thought of it. "I really am. It's a little warmer here than I'm used to, but the countryside is very pretty."

"Have you been to the grove yet? Just beyond the glade where the compound is being built."

"The grove?"

"It's this beautiful little part of the forest sheltered by the trees; there's a small little river, and the sunlight seeps in in this one particular spot. I love resting there. I'd take you, but...my sisters spend a lot of time there, too. We'd have to go when they're not around," she said.

"When are they around?" he asked curiously.

Freja pondered. "Well, we sleep there, but we leave at dawn most days and come back around noon."

Danford laughed a little. "Oh, I was gonna say maybe we could go right now."

A flicker of excitement gleamed in her eyes. "Well...there's also the dell. My sisters don't know about it. It probably looks so beautiful at night."

His heart fluttered again, and it felt like there were a thousand butterflies racing around inside him. "O-only if you're up for it," he said shyly. "I know it's late."

She smiled at him and said, "The later the better, right? There'll be no one around to disturb us."

Her words intensified the fluttering, butterfly feeling. "Th-that's true," he replied.

Freja got up, holding Danford's hand firmly as she pulled him out of bed with her. "Come on," she said excitedly, heading for the door.

"O-okay," he stammered, following behind her as she led the way out of his room and through the corridor. Although he was nervous as hell, he was happy that she was spending time with him. Maybe his feelings weren't stupid, maybe Freja really did like him. But he didn't want to think about all of that right now. He just wanted to see where she was taking him and enjoy what time they'd get together.

Chapter Ten

➤─ ☽ 🍎 ☾ ─≪

The Dell

Freja led Danford off the galleon and down to the shipyard. They stuck to the shadows, heading to the icy Citadel roads; the moonlit streets were silent, and for the first time since he'd left the portal island, he saw skyfish. Silvery, bass-like fish with gleaming red fins swam around the gas lamps lined along the roads, and something *huge* moved through the few scattered clouds above.

Once they reached the tree line, Freja shifted effortlessly into her beautiful golden-furred wolf form. Danford followed suit, his own sandy-brown fur feeling dull in comparison. He couldn't help but admire her, though—her coat gleamed under the moonlight like something ethereal, every strand catching the light as if it were spun from pure gold. Her fur shimmered like expensive silk, flowing with a natural elegance that made him think, just for a moment, that if gold could be reeled and sewn into a blanket, it would look like this— soft, rich, and untouchably beautiful. He couldn't take his eyes off her.

"This way," the Luna said, keeping her voice hushed. She turned around and hurried into the woods, looking back over her shoulder.

Danford followed her, his paws barely making a sound against the soft snow, his heart racing—not just from the anticipation of where she was taking him, but from the simple fact that he was with her. Every time she turned her head to glance back at him, her golden eyes shimmering like two burning stars, he felt a pull he couldn't quite explain. He was admittedly anxious about getting caught; he didn't want to get into trouble. But no one was awake at this hour, not even Greymore.

The trees around them swayed gently, the leaves whispering secrets to the night air as they moved deeper into the woods. The moonlight filtered down through the branches, dappling the forest floor in patches of silver, blue, red, purple, and gold. Danford kept close to Freja, his eyes flicking between her graceful form and the path ahead, though he had no idea where they were going. All he knew was that he would follow her anywhere.

As they weaved through the moonlit woods, the scent of pine and damp earth filled his nose, mingling with the fresh, crisp night air. Freja moved confidently, her steps light as if the forest itself bent to her will, guiding her. Danford could sense something different here; every shadow seemed to dance with life, every breeze carried with it a promise of something beautiful just beyond sight.

Then, suddenly, the trees parted, and as they emerged into a stunning dell, Danford's breath caught in his throat.

The moonlight bathed the dell in a soft, ethereal glow, making the wild grasses and flowers shimmer as if coated with stardust. A small, crystal-clear stream wound its way through the centre, reflecting the moons like a river of stained-glass. The trees that framed the dell were ancient and towering, their branches swaying gently as if bowing to the beauty of the night. The whole place felt untouched, pure—like a secret hidden away from the world.

Freja paused at the edge of the dell, turning to look at him with a smile, her fur gleaming. Danford stepped forward, his gaze sweeping over the beauty before him. He had never seen anything like this before. It felt surreal, like stepping into a dream he didn't want to wake from. The air here was cleaner, softer, almost enchanted.

"Oh, wow…this is beautiful," he said—he wished he had a better way to explain it—as he padded closer to her, his heart swelling with a mixture of awe and something deeper, something he wasn't sure he could name. Freja led him here, to this place, as if she were sharing a part of herself with him. And for that, he was more than grateful. "And…warm," he added, glancing behind him; while the woods were thick with snow, the small opening had only small amounts of frost.

"It's the water," Freja said as she began walking towards it. "The humans call them hot springs, but this one has nothing to do with whatever's happening underground."

Curious, Danford followed her to the water's edge.

She reached in and moved the shimmering sand-like dust from the bottom of the gently flowing stream, revealing a *massive*, glowing purple crystal surface. "It's a void gem. There's stories about how these are the actual crystals that form at the very bottom of Aegisguard, separating it from the Underworld and whatever else is down there; sometimes, the crystals grow a lot bigger than usual, and they can be found under the ocean—or, if we're lucky, rivers and streams," she explained, watching as the sand slowly formed back over the crystal, hiding it from view. "They're warm because of all the ethos inside them."

Danford gawped at her for a moment, every word fascinating him once again. He loved hearing her voice, but he also loved that she knew so much about this world. Of course, he had a million questions, and he didn't really know where to start. So he looked down into the water again and began with, "Can we touch it? The crystal."

Freja smiled almost suggestively at him. "If you like."

"Is…it safe?" he asked nervously.

She nodded. "Yeah."

"O-okay…" he said unsurely. But then he glanced at her and said, "We have to do it together."

The Luna giggled. "Okay." She eased her paw back into the water.

Danford did the same, and then together, they moved their paws closer to the bottom of the stream. Before their paws reached the sand, though, Freja laughed and abruptly jumped on him, pulling him into the warm water with her.

"Hey!" he exclaimed as they splashed around; the water wasn't very deep—it reached up to his stomach—and as they playfully fought, the sand beneath them shifted, revealing the crystal and lighting the dell a dim violet.

Freja stopped to stare around, the purple shimmering in her dark pupils. "It's so beautiful," she drawled.

He couldn't help but admire her once again. But this time, she caught him, catching his gaze before he could look away.

"What?" she asked softly.

Danford wanted to dismiss the question, but…that small, brave part of him urged him to say something *finally*. "You're just…really beautiful," he said, looking at her neck to avoid the deep, enthralling gaze of her eyes. "Even without the light, you're the prettiest girl I've ever laid eyes on," he added embarrassedly.

"Really?" she asked, sounding surprised.

"Yeah, like…when moonlight hits a valley just right, but not just any valley; this one's…full of golden flowers," he said shyly, slowly lifting his gaze to meet her eyes. "And it feels like home—like the only place I want and need to be." As he saw an adoring smile appearing on her face, he looked away again. "I don't know, I just—"

"You just…what?" she asked almost desperately, staring at him.

He felt like he was crazy because he liked her so much but they'd barely known each other very long and only shared a handful of moments…but he wanted to be with her forever. No normal person would think that so soon, though, and they especially wouldn't say it out loud. However, he knew that he was infatuated with her, and it was hitting him so hard because she was interested in him, because she was nice and beautiful. "I just really like you, Freja," he finally said.

She stepped a little closer to him. "I really like you, too, Danford."

His heart raced in his chest. "You're not just saying that, are you?" he asked.

Freja shook her head. "No. Why would I lie to you?"

He sighed a little and looked away. "I don't know. I think people think it's funny sometimes," he said despondently.

With a sorrowful frown, Freja gently nuzzled the side of his muzzle as if to kiss him. "I'd never lie to you. I have no reason to."

It wasn't the first time he'd heard that and still been used, ridiculed, and disposed of. But…he chose to trust her. Something inside him urged him to surrender despite the desire to keep his defences up, so he did. He believed her words, and he hoped that he wouldn't find himself regretting it. "Thank you," he murmured sadly.

She then ushered him out of the stream and onto the warm grass, sending ripples of glittering dust into the air around them as she slumped down with him. "Do you want to stay here with me?" she asked him. "Just for tonight. I don't want to go back to the grove. My sisters all have their lovers, and I'm just…alone," she mumbled, pouting sadly as she looked away.

"Of course," he answered. He didn't want her to feel sad, and if he was the person she wanted with her, he felt honoured.

Freja smiled at him and rolled onto her back. "At least the clouds are clearing up," she said, the stars reflecting in her eyes. "I was afraid it might rain."

"If it does, at least we can sneak back inside," he said, laying on his back, too.

She groaned and laughed amusedly. "I find it hard sleeping inside," she mumbled. "I've been sleeping in the woods my entire life; it just feels…weird."

"I used to ask to sleep outside a lot growing up, but my parents never let me," he said with a light chuckle. "They were worried about bears and stuff."

Freja giggled. "Bears? What's a bear to a werewolf?"

"Well, *now*, not much, but quite a lot for an eight-year-old."

She turned her head and smiled at him. "My parents had me fighting bears at *five*," she said with a smirk, almost as if she was teasing him.

He laughed, too. "Oh, wow. I think when *I* was five, the only thing I was fighting was a sugar addiction."

Amused, she laughed and rolled onto her side, facing him. "What was it like? Growing up in a human household with all the struggles and problems that come with being a young werewolf? When I hit puberty, it was *not* pretty," she said, grimacing and shaking her head.

Danford shrugged. "Hard," he answered. "And frustrating at times. But they educated themselves as much as they could and really did their best. I think that's part of why I don't really get along with everyone else; I'm too…human-y…or something. Everyone can kinda tell."

"I couldn't," she said. "Well…I knew that there was something different about you, but in a good way. You weren't loud and annoying and trying so embarrassingly hard to impress me. You kinda just…keep to yourself, and I like that. Unlike the others, you're not spending almost all of your time trying to pretend you're something you're not."

"I just don't really have werewolf-y aspirations most of the time, and it's hard for some people to wrap their heads around, I think. Not that I think I'm better than everyone for it, though."

The Luna smiled again. "In my eyes, you *are* better than everyone else. You should be proud of it, you know; not every wolf can say they have something that makes them different from every other wolf out there."

"Maybe one day everyone else will agree," he said amusedly.

She rolled onto her back again. "Probably not. Difference unsettles people, especially those who have no desire to try and understand that not everyone thinks, feels, or does the same things."

Instead of a proper response, Danford let the words slip from his mouth as he lightly sniffed the air, "You smell really nice."

Freja giggled once more, turning her head to look at him. "You smell really nice, too."

"Not as good as you, but thank you."

Something then flickered across the Luna's face—curiosity mingled with shyness, perhaps. "Can I ask you something *really* personal?" she asked him, hiding her brief expression with an amused, playful smirk.

He was nervous—of course he was. But he nodded.

"Have you ever had sex in your wolf form?" she asked without hesitation.

If he were in his human form, he was sure that his face would be as red as the crimson moon. "N-no...have you?"

"No," she answered and shuffled closer. "I think we should change that."

His heart started racing again. "R-right now?"

She nodded.

"Okay," he said nervously.

Freja's sweet smile sent a shiver down Danford's spine as she edged closer, her golden eyes flickering with something that made his heart thump *hard*. When she nuzzled against his neck, her warm breath tickling his fur, he tensed, but it wasn't from anxiety—it was anticipation. As she slowly stroked her muzzle up, grazing the sensitive skin beneath his fur, his body reacted on instinct, leaning into her touch, pressing his nose into the soft, intoxicating warmth of her coat.

Her scent—wild and inviting—flooded his senses, overtaking him, making every nerve come alive with desire. It wrapped around him, replacing every trace of doubt with a burning need. Freja's touch was deliberate, slow, and torturous in the most thrilling way. He breathed her in deeply, his heartbeat thundering in his chest, the last of his restraint crumbling.

The desperation in him grew stronger with every moment, his blood pounding through his veins as he edged closer. The need to feel more, to have her, consumed him. His mind raced, but his body had already made its decision. He wanted her—no, he needed her—and there was no stopping the hunger now coursing through him.

Danford's lips parted, his breath catching as he nuzzled back, a groan of longing escaping him as he moved in closer. He wasn't going to wait any longer—this moment, this overwhelming pull between them… it was too powerful to resist.

Wordlessly, Freja turned, her movements smooth yet laced with the same desperation that was coursing through Danford's veins. She leaned forward into the soft grass, her golden fur shimmering under the moonlight as she parted her back legs, the silent invitation clear. Her bushy tail swayed side to side, teasing him, almost like a hunter's lure—except this time, Danford was more than willing prey.

His breath quickened as the sight of her sent a surge of hunger through him. The soft, deliberate sway of her tail made his pulse race, a tantalizing signal he couldn't ignore. Freja let out a quiet, longing whine, and that was all it took. He stepped forward, closing the distance between them, his body pressing eagerly against hers.

As his crotch brushed against her tail, a thrill shot through him, his instincts fully taking over. He positioned himself over her, his desire overwhelming every other thought. The warmth of her body beneath his sent a deep growl rumbling in his throat, and for a moment, he hesitated, savouring the delicious tension hanging between them.

But the moment was brief—he couldn't hold back any longer. The need, the want, the pull… it was all too strong. He moved in closer, his breath hot against her fur as he let his body take what it craved, the longing in her soft whine fuelling his every move. With a long, pleased moan, Danford eased his dick inside her, and Freja's delighted wince urged him to push deeper.

He moved slowly, deliberately, feeling every inch as he pushed his length deeper inside her. Her hot, tight walls gripped him, enveloping him in a way that made him groan with satisfaction, the heat and pressure overwhelming his senses. As she clenched around him, a rush of pleasure surged through his body, pulling a louder groan from his chest.

The connection between them felt electric—every small, intimate detail they shared seemed magnified. He could feel her heartbeat, the way her body responded to his, and it drove him wild. Their breaths mingled, ragged and heated, and when they moaned together, it was like they were perfectly in sync, their bodies moving as one.

Each movement, every sensation deepened the growing bond between them, as if the world around them faded away. All that mattered was the way they fit together—the warmth, the friction, and the raw, pulsing desire that consumed them both.

Danford slowly pulled back, and then he thrusted deep and hard, their moans still entwining. The pleasure was strangely more enthralling, much more overwhelming than any time before—was it because they were in their true, wolf forms, or because Danford… was falling in love with her?

He didn't want to let himself overthink. With a shake of his head and another deep push, he groaned in delight and picked up the pace. Freja's moans grew thicker with sheer satisfaction and delight—there were even hints of surprise and confusion in her whines. She sounded like Danford felt: enthralled, overwhelmed, approaching his peak mere minutes after entering her. But he held on, thrusting, growling, *whining* as the pleasure devoured him whole.

The words tried to escape his lips; his wolf, his heart, his very *soul* urged him to tell Freja that he loved her, that he wanted to be with her forever. But he bit his tongue, refusing to speak confessions that might drive her away. He'd not risk losing her. No, he'd make the most of every moment he got with her.

As a desperate whine escaped Freja's ragged breaths, Danford felt her walls throbbing around his dick, pulling him in deeper as the warmth of her climax teased the tip of his shaft. He let out a pleased whine, glad to know that he'd made her orgasm, and knowing so urged him so much nearer to his own limit.

The moment he felt the end of his shaft swelling, he went to pull out, but Freja clenched *hard* and whined.

"Cum in me," she pleaded, looking back at him. "I want it."

She didn't need to ask twice. Her words sent an utterly consuming desire spiralling through Danford's trembling body, a desperate yearning for satisfaction, a longing to please the wolf he'd fallen for. And as she asked, he plunged his dick deeper inside, letting its end swell, locking their bodies together, and then he climaxed, letting out a relieved, pleased cry as his shaft throbbed.

Freja moaned in relief and satisfaction. Under her panting breaths, she murmured, "Yes, yes."

Danford slowly relaxed as the enthralling pleasure settled inside him. He rested his body on Freja's, calming as she lay down, both of them sighing deeply. But the lingering contentedness quickly faded as the warmth of both their climaxes soaked the tip of his shaft. For their sake, he hoped that she wouldn't end up pregnant, especially since their relationship was extremely new. He worried what her sisters might think of her... and what everyone else might think if they learned that he, Danford, the introverted, human-raised Upsilon had gotten the pack's Luna pregnant. He didn't want anyone to look down on her because of him. And the last thing he wanted right now was children.

His racing thoughts were cut short when he felt Freja move beneath him. He carefully pulled his shaft from her, and when he lay beside her, she shuffled closer and cuddled up to him, resting her head over the top of his.

"I think I like it better as wolves," the Luna said with a quiet laugh.

As he sunk into her embrace, Danford smiled and nervously said, "The primal aspect is nice, but... I think I just like having sex with you in general."

"Me too," she said quietly, a hint of fatigue in her voice. "Maybe we should make a habit of it."

"I'd like that," he said contentedly. "I-I'm not saying that's all I want, though," he assured her, glancing up at what he could see of her face. "We don't have to have sex, I just…like spending time with you."

Freja laughed softly and nuzzled his head. "I know. I like spending time with you, too."

Danford smiled, his heart brimming with a quiet, overwhelming happiness. Freja's embrace, the warmth of her words, her very presence—it all wrapped around him like the softest blanket, soothing every part of him that had ever felt out of place. The sense of belonging she gave him was almost dizzying, leaving him reeling in the best possible way. He knew the thought that he might be crazy would always linger somewhere in the shadows of his mind, but right now, none of that mattered. He wasn't just falling in love with her—no, he had already fallen, and there was no denying it anymore. How could he not love her? Every time he looked at her, it was like his soul was pulled toward hers, irresistibly drawn as if she were a radiant, golden lily and he the honeybee, endlessly searching for the perfect bloom to call home.

Every moment with her was like sinking deeper into an endless pool, one he had no desire to escape from. He was helplessly, hopelessly lost in her, and the more he tried to hold back, the deeper he fell. He wanted her in every possible way—needed her with a desperation that seemed to swell inside him with each passing glance, each brush of her touch.

And *God*, he hoped—he prayed with every fibre of his being that she felt the same, that she wanted him with the same intensity that consumed him. If she did, he knew his heart would never belong anywhere else.

Chapter Eleven

✦— ☽ 🜛 ☾ —✦

Suspicions

| Sunday, Primis 1ˢᵗ, 960(TG)—Nefastus |

anford woke with a light flinch as a cool drop of rain splashed against his cheek. He blinked his eyes open, greeted by the soft, muted light of early morning. The world around him was bathed in a gentle, silver glow, the first hints of dawn barely touching the horizon. The air felt crisp, fresh with the remnants of night, as dewdrops clung to the frost-tipped grass and the delicate petals of the flowers.

He reached out, his human hands brushing against the dusty flora, unsettling the powdery layer from their petals as he searched instinctively. But Freja wasn't there. His fingers grasped at nothing but frost, glittery pollen, and warm earth. When he sat up, his heart sank, the contentment that filled him hours before vanishing like the morning mist.

The dell, which had felt like a sanctuary beneath the moonlight, now seemed cold and empty without her. His eyes scanned the quiet clearing, the trees standing tall but offering no sign of where she had gone. Freja had disappeared without a trace…again.

Despair settled into his chest like a heavy stone. He should've known—should've expected this. Yet every time she left him, it felt like he was losing a piece of himself. The beautiful, fleeting moments they shared always seemed to vanish with the dawn, leaving him alone in the cold light of morning.

But he tried to look at it from Freja's point of view. Her sisters would be expecting to find her at the grove when they woke, and just like him, he was certain that the Luna was trying to avoid suspicions. After all, they were *both* in this…could he call it a relationship? Whatever it was, the two of them were involved, and they both had to evade any suspicions.

He took a deep breath, recovering his sunken heart, shoving aside the negative thoughts. Last night, he'd chosen to trust Freja, he'd chosen to trust every word she told him, and she'd said that she liked him, she'd said that she enjoyed spending time with him, and she'd suggested they even make their meetings a regular thing. *That* was what he wanted to focus on.

However, as his senses slowly woke with him, he caught the smell of cooking meat wafting through the woods—cooking, smoking *pork*. The sweet, tantalizing scents of doughnuts and bread followed, along with the fruity aroma of alcohol. It was the first day of the new year, and he was late to the morning celebration.

Danford's heart sank again as he scrambled around, grabbing his torn clothes; he pulled on his trousers, and although one leg was almost completely shredded, they still covered his crotch—that was all he really cared about. Then, he darted into the snowy woods, racing as fast as his legs would carry him.

When he got to the Citadel streets, there weren't many people about—the odd smoker or dog walker, but everyone else was inside celebrating the new year in Aegisguard's way. Danford wasn't familiar with it, but he was certain that he'd learn all about it from the Aegisguardian wolves once he got back to the ship.

He sprinted through the shipyard, coming to a slow halt as he approached the galleon, but once he climbed the steps and reached the deck, he was met with several suspicious, judging stares.

"Oh, look who decided to join us," Lemuel derided.

"Get lost in the woods?" Nelson teased with a chuckle.

Danford didn't have time to think up a lie. He saw the crowd moving aside, giving way like a towering galleon cutting through a gathering of rowing boats, and from the huddle emerged Greymore. The Alpha loomed over Danford like a spectre, an expectant and irritated glare on his face.

"Where were you?" Greymore questioned. "And what the hell are you covered in?" he added, brushing his hand over Danford's shoulder, wiping away the flower dust.

To Danford's relief, the dust was likely masking Freja's smell—but he had to think fast. "H-hunting," he said and fiddled with his eyepatch. "I thought…well, since I became Upsilon, I'd give a solo hunt a go."

Lemuel scoffed and guffawed. "Clearly, it didn't go well."

Clara slapped his arm. "Shut up."

Greymore sighed deeply, wiping his hand on his shirt. "You know the rules, Danny. You're meant to have a teacher. Anything coulda happened to you out there and no one would've known."

Danford hung his head in shame. "I-I know. I'm sorry. I won't do it again."

"Ugh, enough," came *Freja's* voice.

Danford lifted his head like a hound called for breakfast. There she was…as radiant as ever, standing by the hog which was roasting over a fire; behind her lay a table packed with cornbread, collard greens, black-eyed peas, grapes, doughnuts, cabbage, seafood, and ring-shaped cakes. Champagne, sparkling wine, punch, cocktails, hot cider, and mulled wine. For a moment, that sense of belonging that Danford felt when he was with Freja intensified—surrounded by the familiar feast that his packmates would share back in Eltaria…it all gave him another little glimpse of what life could be like, a glimpse of home—a true, *real* home.

"Come on," she continued and tossed a few grapes to Greymore. "Quit being a boss for the day. It's New Year."

Greymore sighed again but tossed the grapes in his mouth. "Yeah, yeah. All right," he said as he turned around and headed back to the cooking hog. "You heard her—get back to it."

The crowd slowly dispersed, returning to what they'd been doing before Danford arrived, and Randy, Eldora, and Fern began playing light folk music.

Danford didn't want to miss the celebration—or the food…or a chance to admire Freja—but first, he needed to change into some new clothes. As he headed down below deck, a smile broke through his nervous frown. Freja had just saved him from a scolding, and he took it as a sign that she cared. He just wished that he could spend the celebration with her; he was likely going to have to keep his distance to avoid suspicions, and that made him sad. But he'd rather deal with the sorrow than the repercussions that would come with the pack learning that he and Freja were sneaking off to have sex.

He stepped into his room, and to his surprise, the izuret was gone, but it left behind a note and a gold-tipped fountain pen on the couch. With a curious frown, he walked over there, and when he opened the note, it just said 'thank you' in very bad handwriting. It made Danford smile, though. Although the izurets could be intruding—among many other things—they were also very sweet. He took the pen and placed it on his table, and he tucked the note into one of the drawers.

As he got dressed, he thought about last night. He thought about everything Freja said to him. It rolled around inside his head, bringing a content smile to his face once more. She was so beautiful, so amazing, so wondering. Thinking about her made him feel like he had butterflies trapped in his stomach; it made his heart race a little faster, it made him stifle his breaths as he tried to contain the sheer happiness.

He grabbed some new clothes, left them on his bed, and went into the bathroom. His shower was short but thorough, washing off the scent of both dusty flowers and his golden-furred lover. Was it wrong to call her that? Probably. Stupid. But…she meant so much to him. Labelling it wasn't a good idea, though, was it? He shook his head and switched off the water.

Once he dried off and got dressed, he tidied his hair, fixed his eyepatch into place, and headed for his door. But before he could reach for the handle, a knock came at the wood, and the floorboards outside creaked quietly. He hoped it was Freja, and he opened the door without thinking—

"Gosh, there you are," Peris said, gleaming at him. She wore a red dress and a grey cardigan, her hair now brushed neat and long. "I saw you stumble up onto the deck, but I didn't manage to catch you before you disappeared."

Danford admittedly felt a little bad. He'd said he'd take Peris to see the city last night, but instead, he'd run off with Freja. But…the Luna meant more to him, and he wasn't ashamed to admit it. He wanted to be Peris' friend, though, so he wouldn't let his desire or preference for Freja's company ruin that. "Oh, yeah, sorry," he said with a chuckle, dragging his hand over the back of his neck. "I just wanted to tidy up and stuff before joining the celebration."

"Interesting tradition," Peris said, turning on her heel and walking beside him as he left his room and shut the door behind him. "Eating the meat and stuff," she continued, walking with her hands behind her back, glancing at him every few seconds. "We never did anything like that. The beginning of the new year was just like any other day."

"It's an Eltaria thing," he told her, heading for the steps that led up to the deck. "Not just a werewolf thing, either. I mean…sure, werewolves have their own little spin to it, like hunting and catching the hog ourselves, making the bread. But…yeah. Eltarian New Year."

"I don't remember much from my time as a human, but we always had doughnuts with breakfast," she said. "My mom even let me have champagne once."

"That sounds good. I haven't had a doughnut in a long time," he said, thinking about all the food waiting up on deck.

Peris smiled at him, and as they walked upstairs, she said, "Well, I was thinking about last night; since we didn't get to look around the city then, I was wondering if maybe we could go after we've had a little food."

"Uh…" he drawled, panicking a little; he didn't want Freja to get angry at him or suspicious, and he also didn't want to wait until tonight to speak to her again. "I'd love to, but I have some stuff I have to take care of today, so let me just see if I have the time," he said and turned around, heading back downstairs.

"What kind of stuff?" she asked curiously, following.

He felt bad that he was going to have to lie to her; he'd prefer not to, but he had to. He'd protect Freja as best he could. "We work very closely with the demons in the Citadel," he said, heading for his room. "Sometimes, I do stuff for their leader."

"Oh…so…you have to do a job now or something?" she asked.

Danford pushed his door open and headed over to his desk. "I'm not sure yet," he answered, taking a piece of paper and the pen the izuret had gifted him. He quickly wrote a message, asking Freja if it was okay to contact her via izuret, and then he summoned one of the small creatures and handed it the message.

"What the heck is that thing?" Peris asked, startled by its appearance.

"Oh, this is an izuret," he said as the izuret chirped. "They're little cat demons. They're pretty cute." He looked at the creature. "Jadis, this is Peris," he said, gesturing to Peris.

The izuret waved with its free hand.

Peris lost her concerned frown and giggled. "Oh. Hi."

Danford then looked at the izuret. "Be as discreet as possible, please."

With a salute, Jadis disappeared to deliver his message.

"Maybe I can like…help you," Peris suggested as Danford headed for the door again. "I'd love to learn what you guys do, especially with the demons."

"Well, their leader prefers to only work with people he's vetted a tonne of times, but it's quite possible that if you prove yourself one day, he'd be happy to have you help," he replied, closing his door behind them.

"Oh…okay," she said with a nod. "I guess I'm just trying to figure out what I'm meant to do around here," she laughed. "Do I just like…wait to be given a task?"

Danford glanced at her intrigued face. "Once the holiday's over, someone will probably give you something to do. But I don't mind helping you find someone to talk to," he offered.

She laughed a little but sounded disappointed. "Are you trying to get rid of me?" she asked as if she were amused, but the sadness in her voice was as clear as the disheartened frown on her face.

"No, not at all," he said as they climbed the stairs. "I'm just not the one who assigns tasks, so we'd have to talk to someone else about it. I'm happy to help you, though."

Peris nodded. "Okay, well…once you're done, could we still see the city?"

He laughed nervously and said, "We'll have to see what the boss says first."

She smiled at him. "Okay."

Once they got up onto the deck, Danford found an empty table and sat down. Peris sat across from him, and although he didn't want to be rude, he couldn't help but glance over his shoulder at Freja. He watched as she laughed with her sisters, smiling, enjoying the food. Seeing her happy made him feel content, but he also wished that he could be over there with her.

"Where did you go last night?" Peris suddenly asked.

He tensed up a little, setting his eyes back on her. "What do you mean?" he asked as casually as he could. After all, she could mean where he had gone after Freja told them to go back downstairs.

She shrugged and said, "I was exploring the ship and saw you running off." She shot a glance over Danford's shoulder. "With um…Luna Freja."

"Oh," he almost gasped, his nervousness increasing. "We got news of a rogue on the outskirts of Greymore's territory, and we thought we'd go look for him, but he's long gone," he lied. "I'm good at finding stuff, so she asked me to go with her."

Peris' eyes widened a little. "Rogue? Do you know what he looks like?" she asked, sounding as if she'd mistaken his lie for a true story, a story that coincidentally aligned with his fabrication.

"Uhh…brown fur…brown…eyes…pretty standard guy. Kinda tall."

"Was he missing half his tail?" she questioned eagerly. "One odd white paw?"

"Uh…" he drawled. "I'm not too sure, actually. The person who spotted him only got a really quick glimpse…. Why?"

She sighed deeply and leaned back in her seat. "About…two years ago now, Ray," she said, frowning sadly. "He left the pack in the dead of night, he said he couldn't take the mistreatment anymore. He and I were the only Omegas left; he was my only friend, actually. He had half his tail bitten off when he refused to kill Gretchen, an Iota who messed up some of the herbs and made someone's infection worse." She huffed and rested her arms on the table. "I hoped that he was still out there, and if he is, well…you guys would help him, right? Bring him into the pack?"

Now he felt guilty. He hadn't seen a rogue out there and knowing that Peris' friend could be in the woods wandering aimlessly made him feel worse. But he had to keep up the façade. "Yeah, of course. We always give people a chance first."

"Maybe now that Orson and Celeste are gone, he'll come looking for me. He has to know by now that our packs joined together," she said, her eyes wide with hopefulness.

"I'll keep an eye out for him for sure," he said with a nod. But now he wanted to find him. He wanted to go out into the woods and hunt for Peris' friend. He'd have to talk to Greymore about it, though. He was sure that his boss would agree to find a wolf who'd fled to escape the atrocities of the Alphas he'd not long defeated. Not now, though. He felt far too nervous about speaking to Greymore so soon after he and Freja snuck off together. No, he'd wait until the celebration was over at least.

Jadis, the izuret he'd sent to deliver a message to Freja, suddenly landed on the table and held out a small piece of paper to him.

"Oh, your demon leader gets back fast, huh?" Peris asked.

"Yeah," he said with a chuckle and unfolded the paper.

Freja's reply told him that it was okay to use the izurets, but they should be careful and space their replies out over at least an hour or so.

"Excuse me," he said to Peris. "I have to reply to this."

She nodded.

Danford got up and went over to the stairs; he followed a few down, and then he took his pen from his pocket. He flipped the paper, finding his original message, and scribbled it out. Then, in the space below, he wrote:

I had a really nice time last night, and I can't stop thinking about you. Thank you for showing me the dell, it was really beautiful. Not as beautiful as you, though.

I know that this is really new, but I don't want to upset you, so I'm just wondering if you'd mind if I showed Peris around the city like I planned to yesterday. I just kinda feel bad that she wasn't allowed to do anything under Orson and Celeste, and she really wants to get out and see things. If that makes you uncomfortable, though, that's totally okay. I understand.

Anyway, I miss you, and I can't wait to meet you again. Maybe tonight?

He then folded the paper up before his nervousness could convince him that he was being too forward. With a deep sigh, he headed back up the stairs and handed the folded paper to the izuret. "Delay a little," he told it.

With a nod, the creature took off and disappeared into a puff of smoke.

"So...new task?" Peris asked as Danford sat back down across from her.

"Nah, I just had to complete a report real quick; I'm still waiting to hear back. Did you have breakfast yet?"

"I had a doughnut, but I'm waiting for the hog to be ready," she said excitedly.

He nodded, glad that she had something to eat. "Who did they make you bunk with?" he then asked.

"Oh, um...two Upsilons, Jenna and Lila. They seem okay. But Jenna snores."

Danford laughed a little. "Just be lucky you're not close to Greymore's room; he snores loud enough to hear outside of the boat some days."

She giggled. "I don't envy Luna Freja, then."

He wanted *so badly* to reveal that Greymore and Freja weren't really together, but he knew that it wasn't a good idea. "Yeah..." he drawled amusedly.

Peris' eyes then shifted to something behind Danford—

"Danford," came Freja's voice.

As he looked up at the Luna, he tensed up, filled with nervousness, relief, and fear all at the same time. "O-oh, hey," he replied as Freja stopped by their table. "What's up?"

"I just had a talk with Greymore; I think that you should take advantage of the empty streets and show Peris around the Citadel. Fern's taking a few of the others," she said, glancing over at Fern, who was gathering up some of the new pack members. "Show her where she'll be allowed to go until she's a higher rank."

Staring at her face, searching for hints of hidden emotion, he said, "Oh...okay."

Freja smiled at Peris—and there it was...hostility. The slightest, tiniest little flicker that said the Luna didn't want this girl near Danford, but to avoid suspicion, it was a necessary compromise. "Danny knows all the backstreets; he'll show you where we go when things get heated, and he'll show you to safe routes we take to get to and from certain parts of our territory."

Peris smiled excitedly. "Okay," she said with a nod. "Right now?"

"Yeah, right now," Freja replied, looking at Danford. "If you're okay with that."

Wide-eyed, he said, "S-sure. Um…." He wanted to say more, but he knew that he shouldn't talk to her too much. "Okay, well…" he said, struggling. Just seeing her this close…hearing her, *smelling* her—he wanted her so bad, but he had to resist his desires. He had to act like he was the obedient Upsilon, and she was his intimidating superior. And he didn't struggle much at that because she still intimidated him, but in a way that he found he was starting to like. "Are you ready?" he asked Peris.

She nodded frantically. "Let's go!" she exclaimed, standing up.

"Be careful," Freja said firmly. "Most of the humans are celebrating in their homes, but some bars are open. You know the rules," she said to Danford.

He nodded and said, "Yeah." But he felt guilty. He knew already that Freja didn't want him hanging out with Peris, but again…they had to do everything they could to keep suspicions at bay. "Are you going out, too?" he asked her.

The Luna shook her head. "Come on. Greymore wants you back by noon."

"Y-yeah, understood," he said as he got up, too.

Freja then turned around and walked off, disappearing into the crowd.

Every time he saw her walk away, his heart hurt. The guilt weighed him down, so much that he considered sending Peris with Fern's group, but he didn't want to be rude. He just wished that he and Freja didn't have to sneak around, stealing glances and using the cover of the early morning hours to spend time together. But he knew that wasn't possible. He just had to take what he got.

With a quiet sigh, he looked at Peris and tried focusing on the task at hand. "Okay, let's go," he said.

Peris excitedly led the way down off the ship.

Danford followed and smiled as best he could through his conflicting feelings. He wished that Freja could go with them at the very least. He looked back over his shoulder, hoping to catch a final glimpse of her, but she was nowhere to be seen. Maybe he'd see her when he got back, or maybe he'd have to wait until tonight—either way, he just wanted to see her again, and if he had to wait until sunset…then he would. The wait was worth it.

Chapter Twelve

→— ☽ ☂ ☾ —↞

Quiet, Icy Streets, and Whispers of History

All Danford could think about while he took Peris through the quiet, icy Citadel streets was Freja. Freja, Freja, Freja. Her beautiful, golden eyes, her perfect, silky fur, her smile, her laugh, her voice. He waited for an izuret to return with her reply, hoping she'd say that they could meet again tonight.

"Wait, so… if things go bad, like someone gets into a fight or something, we use *that* alleyway to get back to the shipyard?" Peris asked, repeating what he'd just told her.

He nodded. "Yeah, and that one takes you to where the new compound is being built," he said, pointing to the alleyway between a closed tavern and a boarded-up storefront. "Once you get used to our pack's smell, though, you'll be able to navigate all the safe passages through scent alone."

Peris nodded, following him as he continued down the cobblestone street. "So, will I be allowed to come here alone?" she asked curiously. "Or do Omegas need someone with them?"

"Well, I think Greymore's going to want somebody with all the new pack members at least for now—you know, until you're all up to speed and used to the territory."

"That makes sense. So, does this mean that you're going to be my chaperone for a while, then?" she asked, almost smirking at him.

He fought through the awkwardness and chuckled lightly. "Maybe," he replied.

She then spun around, her eyes darting up and down the street. "Can we find an open store or something? It's been so long since I got to go into a shop."

"Yeah, of course. I don't think many will be open today, but you never know."

They trailed the streets, passing only a few open bars with one or two people inside. Danford was close to suggesting they head back and try again later in the day, but when they turned onto Newbury Street, glowing light came from just one building on the long, winding street. They moved closer, and when Danford saw that it was an antique store, he stopped outside and glanced at Peris.

"Some elves have this kind of tradition," he started, taking his eyes off her to look inside the large windows, eyeing all the antique furniture and trinkets stuffed inside. "They give one thing from their home to stores like this and trade it for something else. Something about...spreading the light and luck of a new year, giving an item that holds memories of the past year and receiving one in return. Sharing memories...I don't really know how they explain it, but...yeah."

"That's sweet," Peris said, smiling widely. "Can we look inside, or it is an elf-only kinda thing?"

"No, we can look inside. Just be careful. Some of the stuff in these places is older than we are combined."

She nodded and waited for him to lead the way inside.

Danford pushed open the heavy wooden door, a faint bell chiming overhead as he invited Peris in first, and then he followed her as she passed and smiled at him. The warm air inside the shop hit him immediately, a welcome change from the chilly, icy streets outside. The smell of aged wood, musty leather, and a faint trace of pipe tobacco greeted him, mingling in the air like the scent of time itself.

His boots scuffed softly against the uneven floorboards as he took his first steps inside, his eyes adjusting to the dim light. The shop was crowded with a haphazard arrangement of furniture and trinkets, each piece seeming to tell its own quiet story. Dust swirled in the slivers of light that seeped through the narrow, fogged windows, making everything feel suspended in time.

Along the walls, shelves sagged beneath the weight of old books with cracked spines, some tied with fraying ribbons to keep them from falling apart. A large, ornately carved clock ticked softly in the corner, its hands moving at a leisurely pace, as if the world outside didn't matter here. The air had the faint scent of old parchment and polished brass, the kind of smell that reminded him of forgotten attics and hidden treasures.

He moved carefully through the clutter as Peris curiously followed, the path winding between tables draped in faded lace cloths, each surface crowded with delicate glassware, tarnished silver candlesticks, and small figurines of animals and people, their painted faces worn from years of handling. A few oil lamps cast a soft, flickering glow over the scene, their light casting long shadows that danced across the walls.

The deeper they went, the more the shop seemed to open up like a treasure trove of forgotten memories. Gilded mirrors leaned against the walls, reflecting distorted images of the shelves behind him. An old cello and violin sat on a sturdy oak table; he imagined the soft, gentle sounds filling the space with the ghost of music from long ago.

His fingers brushed against the smooth wood of an intricately carved cabinet as he walked by, the grain cool and worn beneath his touch. A large globe sat on a pedestal nearby, its faded continents showing the world as it once was. The scent of beeswax polish lingered faintly, mixing with the ever-present dust and the sharp tang of metal from the nearby display of old tools and keys hung carefully on rusted hooks.

Danford found himself drawn to a small, glass display case at the back of the shop, where a collection of pocket watches lay nestled on a velvet cushion. The ticking from the clock seemed to grow louder as he stared down at them, each one a delicate reminder of time passing, slipping away like the quiet moments spent in the dusty, forgotten corners of life.

It was as if the shop existed outside of time, a place where the past lingered, waiting to be discovered again. And as Danford stood there, taking it all in, he couldn't help but feel a strange connection to it, as though the weight of history rested in the air, pressing gently against his chest.

"I *love* these," Peris said, admiring one of the pocket watches. "My dad used to have this silver one; I remember he had our names carved onto the back of it."

"That one's cute," he said, pointing to one shaped like the face of a fox.

Peris giggled. "Aw."

"Can I help you with anything?" came an old man's croaky voice.

Danford turned to face the old elf. "Not at the moment; we're just looking around. Thank you, though."

With a nod, the elf turned around and disappeared among the forest of ancient furniture and trinkets.

Something gold shimmered in the corner of Danford's eye, and when he turned in its direction, he spotted a glass display case filled with jewellery. "I'll just be over here," he said to Peris, who nodded. He headed to the case and looked inside at all the necklaces, earrings, rings, and lockets. But one gold locket in particular caught his attention. It had a very thin chain with a heart pendant, and connected to it was a constellation that looked similar to Aries, the very constellation that he and Freja had met under.

He wanted to get Freja a gift, and the locket seemed perfect. So he carefully picked it up and made his way to the counter that the old elf was sitting behind. "Um, hi," he said.

The man looked up and smiled. "Did you find what you were looking for?" he asked as he stood up.

Danford placed the locket on the counter. "Just this, please," he said.

"Of course. One moment," the elf said, taking the locket.

With a nod, Danford watched the shopkeeper disappear into the shadowy room behind the counter. The door creaked shut with a soft thud, leaving him alone in the stillness of the shop. His gaze drifted over his shoulder, scanning the crowded space until he spotted Peris. She was standing near the far corner, her fingers brushing the keys of an old piano as though she were coaxing a long-forgotten melody from it. The instrument, though worn, retained an air of quiet dignity, its once-polished wood now dulled by time and dust.

Danford's curious eyes followed the lines of the piano upwards, where the shelves mounted on the walls were packed with clutter, each piece vying for space. A haphazard collection of oddities filled the room—porcelain vases with faded floral patterns, old brass candelabras with half-melted candles, and the glint of tarnished silver teapots tucked into forgotten corners.

And then his eyes caught on something else—the mirrors.

They lined the walls like silent sentinels, their gilt-edged frames dulled with age. Some were small, no bigger than a hand, while others stretched tall and imposing, their glass fogged with the passage of years. A few had cracks spiderwebbing across the surface, distorting the reflections within. He stepped closer, feeling the weight of the stillness, and glanced at his own faint reflection in one of the smaller mirrors, the glass so tarnished that his face was little more than a shadow.

But it was the picture frames beneath the mirrors that truly held his attention. Rows of them, each unique, lined the shelves, some upright, others stacked in uneven piles, waiting to be rediscovered. He leaned in, his fingers caressing the rough edges of one frame that stood out—its once-golden surface was peeling, the ornate carvings of leaves and vines worn down by years of handling. It was empty, the space where a photograph or painting once rested now a hollow void, as if the memories it once held had slipped away with time.

Another frame caught his eye, larger and heavier, its deep mahogany wood gleaming faintly under the dim light. The glass inside was cracked, splintering the portrait of a stern-looking man into fragmented pieces. His dark eyes seemed to follow Danford as he moved, a reminder of lives long past, preserved in delicate strokes of ink and paint. The frame itself was thick, almost overwhelming in its solidity as if it had been built to hold something much more significant than just a simple portrait.

Some frames were simpler—thin, delicate wood polished smooth by the years. They were stacked with care, their faded corners peeking out from beneath heavier, more elaborate pieces. Others had intricate carvings—swirls and curls that danced along the edges like forgotten artwork. One particularly fragile frame, covered in a layer of dust so thick it almost looked like it was part of the wood, housed an old daguerreotype of a woman in a high-necked gown, her face serious and her eyes haunting.

Danford ran his thumb over the surface of one smaller frame, its bronze finish cool to the touch. Inside, a painting of a young couple stared back at him, their faces frozen in time, smiles just barely touching their lips. It stirred something in him, a pang of nostalgia for a life he hadn't lived, for moments he hadn't been a part of. The past seemed so close here, tangible, as if he could reach out and grasp it, only to feel it slip through his fingers like sand.

Every frame, every mirror, every object seemed to whisper of forgotten stories, of lives once lived and moments long gone. And as Danford stood there, surrounded by the echoes of history, he felt the weight of it all pressing down on him, making him wonder how many stories had been left untold, locked away in the dusty frames and cracked glass of this old shop.

And in his wondering, his eyes found something else, something that grasped his attention more than anything else in this beautiful, wonderful place. Tucked beneath a larger, imposing frame was a delicate, oval-shaped one, about the size of a book. It gleamed softly in the low light, a warm golden hue standing out against the dustier objects around it, and he felt an inexplicable urge to reach for it, like instinct.

As he lifted the frame carefully from its place, his breath caught for a moment. The gold was intricately detailed, delicate vines twisting around the edge, tiny roses blooming in perfect, frozen stillness. The craftsmanship was so fine, so elegant, that it reminded him instantly of Freja—how she moved with that same grace, her presence commanding yet somehow gentle, like the roses in his hand. The longer he stared at the frame, the more vivid the comparison became. Freja's golden fur flashed in his mind, gleaming beneath the moonlight, just as this frame shimmered softly, catching the faint light in the room.

His fingers traced the delicate floral patterns, feeling the intricate carvings beneath his skin. The roses, so finely detailed, made him think of how Freja carried herself—beautiful, yet with a kind of strength woven into her every movement. Even when she was still, she radiated a quiet power, much like this frame. It was as though someone had captured her essence in gold and roses, preserving it in a way that he could hold in his hands.

Danford's thumb moved slowly along the vines that curled around the frame, their endless loops reminding him of the way he felt about her—an unbreakable pull, a connection that wound tighter with each passing moment. The vines mirrored how he felt tethered to her, even when she wasn't near, a part of him always reaching out for her, unable to let go.

He turned the frame over in his hands, its weight comforting yet gentle. It was empty, the space where a picture should have been long since abandoned. But even in its emptiness, it held a kind of promise—like something precious had once been there, and something even more meaningful could take its place. His mind wandered, imagining a drawing of Freja held within this golden frame, her radiant smile captured forever in that perfect, eternal bloom.

A soft sigh escaped him as he stared at the roses again, the way they curled in perfect formation. They made him think of how his feelings for her had blossomed, slowly at first, but now they had grown so intense it sometimes overwhelmed him. Every time he looked at her, he fell a little more deeply, like he was sinking into something far bigger than himself, something as beautiful and untouchable as the frame in his hands.

He found himself thinking about the way she made him feel—how she filled the empty spaces in his heart, the way this frame had once cradled a cherished memory. The hollow inside the frame seemed to mirror the part of him that had always felt alone, but with Freja, it was as if that emptiness was slowly being filled. He wanted to keep her close, like a picture held in this frame, always there, always present.

Danford's grip on the frame tightened, a sudden, strange longing swelling in his chest. He couldn't quite understand why such a simple, unassuming object stirred something so deep within him, but it did. Perhaps it was the way the frame seemed to mirror his feelings for Freja—delicate yet strong, beautiful yet fragile, filled with the untold potential of something precious. He didn't need a picture of her to keep her close—she was already there, woven into the very fabric of his thoughts, as intertwined with his heart as the roses and vines that encircled the frame. But an overwhelming desire overtook him. He wanted to capture her, to sketch every perfect detail of her face, her form, her presence. He wanted to enshrine that beauty within this frame, to seal it forever and gift it to her—a token of everything she meant to him, something she could hold and know she had become the very centre of his world.

He took the frame to the counter and placed it down, waiting for the elf to return.

And just seconds later, the old man stepped out from the room and smiled at Danford as if something he'd been expecting to happen had just happened. "I see you found your trinket," he said, placing the wrapped locket on the counter.

Danford frowned and looked down at the picture frame. "My trinket?"

The elf nodded. "Everyone who comes into this place has something waiting for them, whether they know it or not. You found yours rather fast; I've stood here and watched people take hours to find what's calling to them."

"Oh…wow," he drawled, intrigued. He then looked over his shoulder to see if Peris had found anything, but she was still browsing. "How much is this and the locket?"

"The frame is free; it is already yours," he said with a bow of his head. "The locket is two coronam."

"Wait, really?" he asked, glancing at the frame.

With a nod, the elf tucked the frame into a paper bag, along with the locket.

As he pulled out a coronam note from his pocket, Danford glanced back to where Peris was. "Um, I'm just gonna see if my friend found anything. One sec," he said, hanging the elf the money.

"Of course. Take your time."

Danford then went over to Peris, who was standing in front of a jewellery case. "Did you find anything you like?" he asked her.

She nodded and pointed to a rose gold necklace with a small golden acorn and oak leaf attached to it. "It's beautiful; it reminds me so much of my mother."

"Did she like acorns?"

Peris laughed a little. "I guess she did. She had a bracelet kinda like this, except it only had the acorn and not the leaf."

"Let's see how much he wants for it," he said, taking the necklace. He then led the way to the counter and placed it down. "How much is this?" he asked.

The elf smiled. "Ah, a beautiful piece of jewellery. This one is five gold."

Danford nodded. "Okay, we'll take it."

Peris squealed excitedly. "Thank you so much, Danny."

"You're welcome," he said as he handed the elf five gold coins. "Enjoy," he then said, handing the necklace to Peris. "It's important to have things to remember family by."

She smiled and put the necklace on. "I love it so much."

"Have a lovely new year," the elf then said, handing Danford his bag.

"You, too," Danford said, and then he began leading the way to the door. He felt content, and he hoped that Freja liked the gifts. But he had to get started on his drawing as soon as he could—the moment they got back to the ship, he'd make a start.

Chapter Thirteen

➤─ ☽ 🐚 ☾ ─✦

Rumours

Moonlight poured into Danford's room, and the party up on deck grew louder. He took his eyes off his drawing, his neck aching as he leaned back in his seat. When his eyes brushed past the clock, he saw that it was 8 p.m. already. How the hell had nine hours passed already?

Drawing had always been so therapeutic for him, but as much as he wanted to continue, he knew that he should probably make an appearance at the party. His hands were dirty with charcoal, though, so he needed to clean up first.

However, for a moment…he just wanted to admire his art, the face of the most beautiful thing he'd ever laid eyes on. He hoped that she liked it, he hoped that she wouldn't be creeped out that he'd drawn her…. With a huff, he dismissed his worry and smiled at his art. It was coming along nicely.

He tidied up his desk a little and then headed into the bathroom. Once he washed his hands and straightened his clothes, he left his room and made his way up to the deck. His packmates were dancing around to the lively music, cheering and laughing; Randy was cutting up what was left of the hog and handing pieces out to people, and Greymore was with the band playing his accordion.

Danford made his way over to the edge while scouring the crowd for Freja. He spotted her standing alone on the forecastle deck, and her sisters were nowhere to be seen. The part of him that craved Freja, the part of him that wanted to be with her all the time urged him to go up there, but *everyone* was on deck, and he didn't want to arouse suspicion. So, as much as it upset him, he stayed where he was.

"Hey," came Peris' voice.

He looked over his shoulder and watched the blonde Omega make her way towards him with a wide smile on her face. "Oh, hey," he said. "Are you having a nice time?"

As she stopped in front of him, she nodded. "I've *never* been to a party like this. Like we had celebrations and stuff, but not like this."

"Yeah, it's pretty great, huh?" he said, and then his eyes drifted back to Freja.

"Where were you all day?" Peris asked curiously.

"Just working on stuff in my room. I'm kind of a recluse sometimes," he answered, glancing at her before setting his eyes back on Freja.

"Why do you keep staring at her?" she snapped.

"I'm not," he insisted nervously, turning his head to look at Peris.

Peris sighed and looked down at the drink she was holding. "I've seen you looking at her," she mumbled sadly. "I've seen the *way* you look at her.

"I-I don't look at her."

"You do, and *she* looks at you." She frowned at him, a mixture of confusion and sadness in her eyes. "Is there something going on with you? Because—"

"No," he exclaimed anxiously.

"—if there is, you *do* know how serious the consequences can be, right? I'm just... worried about you. You're the only friend I have here, and I don't want to see you hurt... or worse."

Danford hadn't actually properly thought about the consequences if he was caught. He knew that the sentence for this sort of thing was traditionally death, but... Greymore wouldn't kill him, would he? *Would he*? He tensed up, looking down at the floor. Maybe they'd banish him. But her sisters... *they'd* kill him, wouldn't they? He felt sick, like he was moments from throwing up.

"And her sisters have been watching you, too," Peris revealed. "I've seen them glaring at you through the crowd several times. I think they're suspicious."

His eyes widened as his anxiety intensified. He tried his best to compose himself and said, "It's probably just a coincidence."

Peris sipped from her drink. "Just be careful, Danny. I don't know what the rules are here, but if this were Orson's pack, the rumour alone would get you killed," she murmured despondently.

"I'm okay, don't worry about it. There's nothing going on, and there's no rumours or anything... right?"

She shrugged. "I've heard her sisters talking. I might not have been the only one; they talk kinda loud."

"What do they say?" he asked worriedly.

Peris moved closer and kept her voice hushed, "The pregnant one said she's seen Freja looking at you, and the other one said she saw you two leaving some Yule party together or something? And they were talking about confronting you or Freja."

He shook his head. "It's all just a misunderstanding, but if you could keep it to yourself, that would be doing me a huge favour."

"Yeah, okay," she said, but she didn't sound entirely convinced.

"Just because you know how rumours go," Danford continued. "People hear something and think its fact, and then they spread it everywhere."

She nodded. "Yeah. Just be careful," she mumbled sadly. "And…I'm here for you, too, if you need to talk."

"Thanks. I appreciate it."

The girl nodded again in response.

Danford smiled lightly, but he couldn't help himself; he glanced around, searching for Freja, hoping for the slightest glimpse of her. When he found the Luna, he saw her effortlessly moving through the crowd. She caught his gaze and smiled suggestively, and then she headed down to the docks. She wanted him to follow, didn't she? He wanted to go, but first, he had to find a way to distract Peris.

He set his eyes on Clara. "Oh, have you met Clara yet?" he asked.

Peris shook her head.

"Come on," he said and started leading her towards Clara. "She's kind of the big sister around here," he explained. He stopped beside Clara, who smiled at him and Peris. "Clara, this is Peris," he introduced. "Peris, Clara."

"It's nice to meet you," Peris said, shaking Clara's hand.

"How are you finding the ship?" Clara asked her.

"Good. I mean I've never been on a boat this big before, so I don't really know what to compare it to, but…it's so much comfier than the forest."

Clara laughed and said, "It certainly is."

"I was wondering if you could help her get set up," Danford said. "Maybe find something for her to do around here?"

"Oh, of course," Clara said with a nod. "What are your skills?" she asked Peris.

"Um…well, I was always very good at tracking," she answered.

"That's a very useful skill."

"I'll be right back," Danford said.

Clara nodded, but Peris looked disappointed. She didn't question him, though; she set her eyes back on Clara, who was telling her how her tracking skills could be helpful.

Danford slinked away. He evaded his packmates' eyes, and he looked around for Freja's sisters, but he couldn't see them—maybe they'd already gone back to the grove. With both excitement and angst racing through him, he made his way down to the docks, following Freja's scent. It led him out of the shipyard and onto the quiet, icy Citadel streets, and when he reached the edge of the city, he saw the golden-furred Luna waiting in her wolf form at the tree line.

He smiled and hurried to her; from his pocket, he discreetly took the constellation locket and put it on his wrist, ensuring it would be safe with him when he shifted. Once he reached the trees, he shifted and stepped into the woods, glancing down at his front ankle to make sure the locket was secure—it was, safe and hidden in his fur.

"Hey," Freja said as she nuzzled his muzzle as if to kiss him.

Danford nuzzled her face, too, and then moved closer, hugging her as best he could with his front leg. "Sorry I took so long."

"Did anyone see you leaving?"

"No, I don't think so. I checked quite a few times."

She smiled and nodded. "Okay, good. Do you want to go to the dell again?"

"I'd really like that," he agreed.

Freja giggled and playfully said, "I'll race you."

"Okay," he said excitedly.

The Luna then turned around and raced into the woods. Danford followed, running as fast as his legs would carry him. Freja was so much faster than him, and when she looked over her shoulder and realized that he couldn't keep up, she purposely slowed down and ran beside him. They smiled at each other, panting as they ran, and when the dell came into view, Freja picked up her pace and leapt into the small, flower-covered glade with a relieved laugh.

Danford jumped over the tree line, too, and when he landed, the stardust resting on the flower petals around him pounced into the air. It covered his and Freja's fur as it slowly settled back down, and then the Luna took him over to the small stream. She sat down, and he sat beside her, gazing at her face, her eyes, her smile. He couldn't look away—he didn't want to.

"I'm sorry I didn't reply to you with the izuret earlier," she said, looking down into the water before setting her eyes on him. "My sisters were clinging annoyingly close to me after I sent you and Peris into the city. I think they're starting to suspect something," she told him, but she didn't sound anxious; she was worried, that was for sure, but there was also a hint of relief in her voice. Why?

"That's fine," he started. "I just didn't want to head out with Peris and upset you. I would have waited all day." But then he thought about what Peris said about Freja's sisters. "Do…your sisters complain about me a lot or something?"

She shook her head and sighed, looking conflicted. "Verity saw us leave Aleksei and Zalith's Yule party the other night. I managed to convince them that you were just showing me some of your drawings, but I think they're still suspicious that there's something going on. They take it upon themselves to remind me at least twenty times a day that I'm an Alpha and I should either try to love Greymore or find another Alpha to date," she explained despondently. "I don't know what it's like with you Eltarian wolves, but here, relationships between Alphas and any rank lower than that are forbidden."

Danford frowned sadly and looked down into the water. "I'm sorry I'm such a burden. I can try to work my way up, but it's just gonna take time, and I feel like I'm gonna get a lot of pushbacks."

Freja moved closer and rested the side of her head on his neck. "I don't want to wait that long," she mumbled. "And this whole rank thing never mattered to me. I don't care."

So why did they have to sneak around? Was she ashamed but didn't want to say it out loud? He didn't want to think about it. He didn't want to sink into despair and let himself overthink. No, he wanted to be happy. He wanted to change the subject. So he lifted his paw and wriggled the locket free from his ankle, letting it hand on the edge of his claws, and then clenched it gently in his paw, keeping it hidden. "I got you something," he said, smiling at her. "But I think you need to be in your human form for it to fit."

The Luna smiled curiously. "Okay," she said, and then she shifted into her human form.

Danford blushed—he couldn't help but stare at her naked body for a moment. He thought he should be a gentleman and do the same, so he shifted into his human form, too. He felt embarrassed sitting there without any clothes, and even more so when he saw Freja looking him up and down with a smile on her face.

He fought through the embarrassment and shyly said, "Turn around."

She turned around, smiling curiously.

With a nervous frown, he placed the locket around her neck and clipped it together. "I hope you like it," he said, pulling his hands away. "It looks kinda like the Aries constellation in Eltaria, the same constellation that we met under—well, the same one we're sitting under right now."

Freja gazed down at the locket, and then she smiled in adoration. "I love it so much," she said softly. "Thank you." She leaned closer and kissed his lips.

He shyly returned her kiss, and then he said, "You're welcome. I saw it at some store, and I had to get it for you."

"It's beautiful," she said as she admired it.

Then, Freja kissed him again, her lips soft but insistent, and then again, each kiss more intoxicating than the last. Danford's heart pounded, every beat sending a rush of heat through him. He barely had a moment to catch his breath before her kisses deepened, and she gently pressed him down onto his back, climbing over him with a graceful ease. The warmth of her body against his was all-consuming, her soft curves fitting perfectly against him as their kisses grew more urgent, more desperate.

Danford's mind raced, nerves stirring just beneath the surface of his desire. He'd never felt this close to anyone before, never felt so exposed and so desperate all at once. But as Freja's hands caressed his chest, as her lips danced over his, his hesitation melted away. Slowly, carefully, he let his hands explore her warm body, feeling the rise and fall of her breath beneath his fingertips. Every touch, every caress brought him closer to her, closer to something he'd only ever imagined.

Her skin was smooth, like silk, warm beneath his hands as he traced the curves of her hips, the arch of her back. Freja let out a soft hum of pleasure, her body reacting to his touch, and Danford's confidence grew. He wanted to make her feel as good as she was making him feel. His hands moved lower, guiding her gently, feeling the way her muscles tensed under his palms.

She pulled back slightly, their lips just barely brushing, her breath hot against his skin. Her golden eyes met his, and for a moment, time seemed to slow. She smiled— something soft yet filled with longing—and Danford knew what she wanted, what they both wanted. He smiled back, then gently, almost reverently, he rolled them over, taking the lead. His hands glided over her body, learning every inch of her as he kissed down her neck, her collarbone, her chest. The sound of her quiet breaths, the slight tremor in her body beneath him filled him with a sense of purpose, of belonging.

Freja let out a quiet sigh as he kissed his way lower, her body arching under his touch. With every kiss, every caress, Danford felt his nervousness fading, replaced by a growing hunger to please her, to make her forget everything else in this moment but him. As he reached her thighs, he gently coaxed her onto her back, guiding her to lie down on the soft grass beneath them. Her legs parted slightly, a subtle invitation that made his heart race.

Danford's gaze travelled over her, admiring the way she looked bathed in the moonlight, her body glowing with warmth and anticipation. He kissed the inside of her thigh, slowly, deliberately, drawing out every moment, every breath. Freja gasped softly, her body tensing beneath him as his kisses grew closer to where she wanted him most. He could feel her anticipation, her need, and it mirrored his own.

With a quiet, content sigh, Danford gently spread her thighs further, settling himself between them. His hands caressed her hips as he lowered his head, pressing his lips to her, tasting her. Freja moaned softly, her body responding to his touch, her legs trembling slightly as he began to pleasure her with slow, deliberate movements of his tongue. He let himself get lost in the moment, lost in her, feeling her every response, her every breath, guiding him deeper into her pleasure.

And in that moment, Danford knew—this wasn't just about desire. It was about the connection between them, something far deeper, something that pulled them together like fate. As his tongue moved over her, and her moans filled the air, he knew he wanted to spend the rest of his life making her feel like this.

He twirled his tongue around her clit, making her moan in delight; he gently sucked it, eased his tongue inside her, and pleasured her until she couldn't take it anymore. She grasped a fistful of his hair and whined loudly as she climaxed, and Danford let out a content hum as he dragged his tongue over her one last time.

Danford then kissed his way back up her body, and when he reached her face, he smiled down at her, and she smiled up at him before she kissed his lips.

But that was when a horrified voice called, "Freja!"

Startled, Danford sharply turned his head in the direction the voice had come from, and when he saw *Verity*, horror struck him. He climbed off Freja as she sat in with a gasp, and he tried to cover up as much of himself as he could with his hands.

"What the fuck, Verity?!" Freja shouted back.

"I knew you were sneaking around with this...this invalid!" Verity yelled. She then shifted into her wolf form and raced into the woods.

Freja panicked. "Wait here," she told Danford before shifting into her wolf form and chasing after her sister.

Danford sat there, watching as she disappeared into the woods. Guilt washed over him, pulling him in deeper and deeper as each moment passed. A part of him wanted to follow in case Freja needed him, but he knew that she could handle herself. But what was going to happen now? Verity had seen them. Would she tell the entire pack? Would Freja have to face the shame and consequences of having a relationship with an Omega-just-turned-Upsilon? He dreaded to think what the next few hours would have in store for her...and for him.

But all he could do for now was sit there...and wait.

Chapter Fourteen

»— ☽ 🜨 ☾ —«

The Luna and the Upsilon

O ver thirty minutes had passed. Freja still wasn't back, and Danford's guilt was quickly being overshadowed by his panic. Had Verity reached the galleon? Was she telling everyone this very moment what she'd seen? Would Greymore and the pack come storming into the dell to issue him his punishment? Or had Freja caught up with her sister and was now trying to convince her not to take the action she had every right to take?

While he waited, he asked himself if he should stop seeing her to save her the trouble that she was obviously getting from her sisters. But he didn't want to stop seeing her. Even the thought of it made him feel sick, like a part of him was being torn away. He couldn't lose her.

He stared into the water, trying to calm his aching heart, but he couldn't dismiss the dismay. What if Freja decided that seeing him was too much hassle? What if she chose her reputation over him? He'd understand if she did, he just wished that for once, he'd be someone's first priority.

The snow beyond the tree line started crunching. He turned his head, looking over there, and when he saw Freja emerge in her wolf form, the urge to run to her struck him, but he stayed where he was when he saw the look of frustration on her face.

"What happened?" he asked worriedly.

Freja slumped down beside him with a huff. "Well, I convinced her not to run to Greymore, but she's going to tell Sophronia and Opal, so all hell is probably going to break loose by tomorrow."

"W-what does that mean?"

"Sophronia will tell Llewellyn, and Llewellyn will tell Greymore—if Llewellyn doesn't tell him, then one of the others will. It's going to spread like a plague," she muttered, sounding hopeless. "My sisters are too traditional to keep this between us."

He felt like he might throw up. "Do you...think they'll kill me?" he murmured.

"I don't know," she said sullenly, looking down into the water. "But the Aegisguardian wolves will be calling for that outcome; it's the way things have always been done here. I don't know how Greymore will handle it, though."

As his fear intensified, Danford took a deep breath, trying to keep himself from panicking too much. He didn't think that Greymore would kill him, but he also didn't know what the outcome would be if Greymore was under pressure to do something. So he blurted, "What if we just run away?"

Freja looked at him. "I was going to say the same thing," she said. But then she sighed, shook her head, and glared into the water. "But we're not kids, and we both know what's waiting for us out there. Even as an Alpha, surviving out here would be impossible. We'd have to leave Greymore's territory, and the only way to do that is to go through the other territories, and if we're not seen and tattled on by one of the packs loyal to Greymore, we'll be hunted and killed by the others. Not to mention the humans outside the Citadel would kill and skin us in a heartbeat." She looked at Danford again. "I don't... know what to do otherwise, though. I thought about going to Greymore before my sisters, but I don't know him well enough to decide whether or not that's a good idea. I mean... if were him, I wouldn't react well to being told that my wife, business marriage or not, was sneaking around with an Upsilon."

He wasn't sure how Greymore would react either, but he didn't believe that he'd want him dead. "I-I can talk to him, I guess. But I don't know how he's gonna react either. I mean he was suspicious after the first night we were together."

She sighed deeply and looked up at the moons. "To be honest, it would probably be better if we both talk to him. He's gonna want both sides of the story." She shifted her gaze back to him. "He's likely drunk as hell from the party, but I don't think we should wait. The sooner we talk to him, the better. I'd rather go now and deal with him slurring words and laughing like an idiot than let my sisters tell him their twisted, stupid little version of all this."

"But what if he gets mad?"

"If he gets mad, he'll be too drunk to do anything but fall on the floor," she said with a roll of his eyes. "He drank enough for the entire pack today."

"I don't know," he drawled unsurely.

"Come on," she said, standing up. "Shift. I don't think my sisters are going to wait until morning."

Although he was so worried that he felt nauseous, he did as she said and got up, shifting into his wolf form. He stood there for a moment, staring at her as she stared back, and as his eyes wandered down to the locket around her neck, he asked himself if he might be walking into a trap. He trusted her... but what if he was making a mistake? What if Greymore was so drunk that he didn't think straight, got mad, and attacked him? Drunk people could be very unpredictable; Danford wouldn't be able to stop him.

He scowled despondently, letting the worry consume him. "What if he kicks me out of the pack?" he asked sadly, staring into her eyes again. "Would you come with me?"

Freja frowned sadly and moved closer. She nuzzled the side of his face and said, "Of course I would."

Danford wanted to believe her, but he'd been in positions before where it was time for people to show up for him and they didn't, so he couldn't fight the worry. And the fact that she seemed okay with putting him in a situation where he might get hurt or worse didn't settle well with him. But he did his best to hide it. "Okay," he mumbled in response. "Thank you."

She then slowly turned around. "Come on. Let's get back."

He nodded and followed her into the woods.

"I should probably do the talking," she said, glancing at him as they hurried back towards the city. "And…I want you to stay behind me, too. If Greymore *does* get angry, I won't let him hurt you. If he asks you anything, answer as best as you can, and try to avoid anything that might trigger him. Again I don't know him so well, but I'd rather him snap at me than you," she tried to assure him.

"I don't think he'd hurt me," he murmured.

"He better not." She sighed deeply and continued, "If he *does* want you gone, then…we can go to Aleksei," she said confidently, staring ahead again. "He'll help us. I think I've done enough to deserve him helping us get somewhere safe."

"I don't know; he doesn't seem to like me very much."

"He doesn't have to like you to do something *I* ask for. It'll be okay," she said firmly.

He nodded, trying to stay calm, but his heart was racing and only grew more frantic the closer they got to the city. There weren't words to describe how nervous he was, or how badly he wanted to suggest they just skip telling Greymore and go to Aleksei first. But he kept his mouth shut, trusting the woman he felt so deeply connected to, holding onto the hope that if he *was* banished, she'd go with him into exile.

When they reached the tree line and followed the Citadel roads, he started trembling, and the contrast between what he felt and the sight and sound of his packmates still partying on the galleon deck was almost harrowing. They were all having fun and didn't have to worry about anything, while he was about to face banishment…or worse.

Once they reached the ship, Freja said to him, "Go and get dressed and stuff. I'll find and take Greymore to that little private lounge on F deck. Meet me there?"

He nodded, and as she disappeared into the crowd, snarling at anyone who got in her way, Danford headed below deck. His racing heart made it hard to breathe—it made it hard for him to shift back right away. He had to take a few moments, inhaling and exhaling slowly and deeply, and when he finally returned to his human form, he fumbled around looking for clothes and one of his spare eyepatches. As he got dressed, though, the panic got worse, like each piece of clothing he pulled on pushed him closer to facing his fate. But he couldn't turn back now—he…*wouldn't*. Freja was the closest thing he'd found to a true sense of belonging, and he wasn't going to give her up.

After a few more deep breaths, he stepped out of his room and *slowly* navigated the ship until he was down on F deck. The terrified part of him wanted to linger, to take his time finding the lounge, but he knew that would only make him feel worse. So he followed the hallway to its end, turned right, and approached the lounge. He could hear Freja and Greymore's voices echoing from the other side of the door, making him tense up even more, but he pushed through.

He took another deep breath and pulled the door open. His eyes found Greymore sitting on one of the couches, and Freja was standing by the window. Greymore's skeptical stare immediately hit Danford, forcing him to look away; he pulled the door shut behind him, and then he stood there like a dog with its tail between its legs.

"So what's going on?" Greymore questioned irritably.

Freja sighed deeply as she moved away from the window. "Before I start, I just want to remind you of our agreement, Greymore."

"Which one?" he asked, watching her as she stood beside Danford.

"The one where we can see whoever we want as long as we keep it discreet."

"Right…."

"Well, Danny and I are seeing each other, and we've managed to keep it a secret until an hour-ish ago."

Danford watched the skeptical stare on Greymore's face turn into an aggravated scowl. He was mad.

Freja continued, "Verity's been suspicious of me since Aleksei and Zalith's party, and she decided to follow me out into the woods tonight. She caught me and Danford together, and I'm certain that she's on her way here right now to tell you and whoever else is around to listen."

"Uh-huh…" Greymore responded, and there was an expectant look accompanying the annoyance and pondering.

The Luna then looked at Danford. "Can I ask you something?" she asked, looking both curious and anxious.

Danford nodded, still trying to hide the dread and anxiety and horror. "O-of course, anything," he answered.

"The other night…when we left the party and came back here, you…you felt it, too…right?" she asked almost desperately, staring into his eyes.

He was sure he knew what she meant, but he also didn't want to assume because he still felt like he was crazy. "Felt what?" he asked but in a way that he made sure Freja would understand was a search for assurance rather than an answer.

She stepped closer, taking hold of his hand. "The connection," she said softly, still gazing at him. "Fate, whatever you want to call it."

Her words made his racing heart flutter for a moment, and the feeling of relief that rained down on him was inexplicable. "I thought I was imagining it," he said, his lips managing to form a relieved but nervous smile.

Freja smiled, too, her face smothered in relief and happiness. But then she turned to face Greymore. "Danford's my true mate, and I have no plans to reject him. So, if us being together means we can't stay here, then we'll gladly go," she told him firmly. "All I ask is that you *let* us go."

Greymore let out a long sigh. "You're really not making this easy for me, Freja," he said, clearly still annoyed—maybe more annoyed than he was a few seconds ago. "You couldn't have picked someone else? No offence, Danny, but you know what I mean."

The Luna scoffed and shook her head. "You know as well as I do that we don't just get to pick and choose who it turns out to be. And even if I could, no; I'd have still gone up to Danford at that party, I'd still have invited him for drinks, and yes, if you must know, I would have still fucked him. He's not like the rest of those loud-mouthed, dick-swinging-contest losers you have partying up on that deck—and you know what? If he was, we'd still be fated." She sounded offended, like *she* was the one who was going to get physical if Greymore said the wrong thing.

"Listen," Greymore said sternly. "If we were back home, I really wouldn't care—and to be honest, I don't care who either of you lie down with—but now that we're all mingled and shit, it makes it more complicated than it should be. I personally don't want either of you to leave, and I really don't think it's necessary, but I'd like you two to explain how you expect to stay here and navigate this relationship of yours amongst potentially hostile company—preferably in a way where I'm not going to have to intervene every twenty minutes."

Freja glanced at Danford, looking like she was thinking. "Everyone knows that our marriage was purely business, even my sisters. I'm sure that it won't come as a shock to everyone that one of us eventually found our true mate."

"But business or not, this marriage is what's keeping our packs together, Freja," Greymore said. "For you and Danny to become mated, we'd have to dissolve our union or unclaim each other or whatever the hell it's called. That shit's going to have everyone up in arms."

"Not necessarily," she snapped, crossing her arms. "Sure, it's a little untraditional, but it isn't always the marriage between Alphas that binds packs. Sophronia married Llewellyn to join Tobias' old pack with mine, and they're both just Betas. If we explain what happened to the pack, if we get them to understand, then everything will be fine. And if it really matters that much, we can just stay married on paper. I don't care about silly human traditions." She frowned and looked at Danford. "Unless…that would make you uncomfortable."

Danford opened his mouth to speak—

"It ain't the paper that matters, Freja," Greymore interjected. "It's the mark, the claim. If the pack is fine with the bond responsible for keeping them together shifting to you and Danford, then sure, whatever, but if they're not, I just…can't see a way for you two—"

"We'll work something out!" the Luna insisted frustratedly.

"When?"

She huffed and tapped her fingers on her arm. "Just…let me and Danny talk about it—give us until the morning. Just entertain that, when they come, my sisters are the first people you're hearing this from," she requested.

Greymore rolled his eyes. "And how am I supposed to react?"

"I don't know, surprised, maybe? Tell them you'll look into it or something that'll convince them that telling you was all they needed to do."

He sighed in response.

Guilt was weighing down on Danford *again*. None of this would be happening—at least not to this extent—if he was just better. "I'm sorry, Freja," he mumbled.

"Why are you sorry? You have nothing to be sorry for," she said firmly, taking hold of his hand again. "We'll figure this out." She glanced at Greymore. "Even if we do have to go to Aleksei."

"Don't bother him with this," Greymore said. "It's werewolf business; he has other things he has to focus on."

"So give us until the morning to figure out what to do," she said firmly.

"I never said I wasn't."

She rolled her eyes. "My sisters are going to be here soon." Then, she asked Danford, "Do you want to head back out to the dell or would you prefer to talk here in your room?"

Danford was still struggling with his emotions—the guilt, the anxiety, everything. "What do you think is best?" he asked, fighting to keep his feelings buried.

Freja sighed. "Probably here since my sisters will likely come looking for us at the dell; I don't want them to ruin that place for us," she mumbled sadly.

"Okay."

She then looked at Greymore as she ushered Danford towards the door. "We'll find you in the morning."

Greymore grumbled something indistinctive and waved them off.

"Oh…uh…Greymore?" Danford asked nervously.

He grunted in response.

"Peris…said something about um…a member of her old pack still being out there somewhere in the forest. Uh…Ray. He's got brown fur…brown eyes…and half of his tail is missing. And he has one odd white paw. I-I told her that I'd keep an eye out for him, but I thought that…well, I thought I'd mention him in case any of the scouts or whoever sees him."

Greymore grunted again, waving them off.

Freja pushed the door shut behind her. Holding Danford's hand, she led the way down the hall. "Are you okay?" she asked quietly.

He shrugged and mumbled, "It's hard not to blame myself."

"It's not your fault. If you want to blame someone, blame the Moon Goddess," she said with a light laugh, clearly trying to lighten the mood. "We don't get to choose who our mates are, Danford. But trust me, we'll figure this out, okay? I promise."

"Weird timing, but you can just call me Danny if you want, I don't mind."

"Okay, noted," she said with another small laugh as they headed up the stairs.

He followed her up, still fighting his emotions. He felt stupid and guilty and small all at the same time, and it all seemed very surreal because it was happening *so fast*. He was one bad conversation away from crying if he was being honest with himself. *Would* he and Freja be able to come up with a solution? Would they be able to stay with the pack while being together, or would they have to leave? He felt as if he'd be fine either way so long as he had her, but he wasn't sure how rogue life would be for Freja. Could she handle it, or was she just pretending to make him happy?

As they reached the top of the stairs, Danford looked at Freja's neck and stared at the locket he'd gotten her. He still hadn't wrapped his head around it all; what he felt the night he and Freja first had sex was real—she *was* his fated mate, and he was hers. He had someone to love, someone to be loved by, but the threat of death or exile was lingering over their heads, leaving him no room to revel in the fact that he'd found his soulmate.

Would they be banished? Would the packs split and fight? Or would the wolves he'd not long come to share a home and territory with call for his beheading? He didn't know, but what he *did* know was that he'd find out in the morning, giving him and Freja less than eight hours to figure out how to keep the pack together…and their heads on their necks.

Chapter Fifteen

≫— ☽ ☕ ☾ —≪

Predicament

While Freja lay thinking beside him, Danford stared aimlessly around his room. His heart was thumping, and his throat hurt every time he took a breath. He tried to think of a way that his and Freja's relationship could work while still remaining in the pack, but nothing was coming to him; his panic, despair, and dismay were all making it impossible for him to think clearly.

A part of him was beginning to sink into the idea that there was nothing they could do. If they wanted to be together, if they wanted to seal the fated connection between them, they'd have to leave, wouldn't they? They'd have to face the world out there as a pair of rogues. And while he didn't mind that fate for himself, he *did* mind it for Freja. She'd been a pack wolf since she was born, and although she told him that she'd leave with him if they had to go, he was almost certain that she'd never be truly happy, that she might even resent him over time for it. He didn't want that. He didn't want to be the reason she had to throw away her entire life.

"I think it would work," Freja said, breaking the tense silence between them. "Our bond being the one that keeps the pack together. As long as Greymore explains everything properly to the pack, I think we could keep them all from kicking off. Greymore and I reject each other's claims, and then…you and I become mated straight after. That way, the pack remains intact."

"What if you end up regretting it, though?" he asked her sadly.

She scoffed amusedly as she turned onto her side, leaning up on her arm to look down at him. "I'm not going to regret any of it, Danny. I've been dreaming about finding my fated mate since I was like sixteen. I watched my sisters find theirs, I watched all my friends find theirs and go off to start their new lives. And now that I've finally found mine, I'm not going to turn my back on him because of pack politics." She placed her hand on the side of his face and caressed it gently. "I want to be with you—here, or out in the woods, it doesn't matter. I just want *you*."

A slither of happiness made its way through the despair. "I just want you, too." He exhaled deeply. "Sorry, I'm not trying to make things harder."

"Stop apologizing," she said. "You have nothing to be sorry for. Everything that's happened and will happen is all for a reason. We just have to trust that the Moon Goddess is doing what she believes is right for us."

With a despondent pout, he moved closer and wrapped his arms around her.

"Do you want to try what I just said or should we think of something else?"

"If you think it's what's best, then I'll do it," he agreed.

She sighed as she caressed Danford's hair. "I can see Greymore's wolves being okay with it because your traditions are different, right? But *mine*...I don't know. I feel like they'd listen to me if I ordered them to accept the change, but my sisters..." she paused and shook her head with a huff. "My sisters are probably going to make a massive fuss, rile the pack up. I thought they'd be happy that I finally found my mate, but they hate the idea of me mating with an Upsilon."

"Why do you let them tell you what to do like this?" he asked sadly.

"I don't let them tell me what to do, I just care about them. They're my sisters; I've grown up with them, and they're just trying to protect me. But I know that in time, I can convince them to understand."

"I understand that, but can't you just tell them to stop? You're the Alpha," he replied despondently.

Freja sat up with a frustrated sigh. "It's not that easy, Danford. Ordering them to stop talking about it isn't going to make them accept it. I love them, and I want them to accept my decision to mate with you—I want them to accept *you*."

"But wouldn't they want to protect you by at least not spreading it around? Peris said that she heard them talking about us and that other people likely heard it, too."

She dragged her hand over her face and huffed quietly. "They're just...too attached to tradition. Whenever this sort of thing happens, when an Alpha's fated mate turns out to be some rogue or an Omega or something, the Alpha is always expected to reject them and either wait out a second-chance mate or marry for business or a pack union. So they're just trying to urge me to stick to tradition." She looked at him and frowned sadly. "Their goal is likely to tell enough Aegisguardian wolves to take action and chase you out—but I won't let that happen, okay?" She took hold of his hand and pulled him into a tight hug. "I'll make my case to them after we've figured out how to keep the pack together."

He exhaled deeply, staring up at her. "I just don't understand why they can't just be happy for you." He looked away as his expression grew thicker with dismay. "Maybe I'm just too used to being a rogue."

"They just need to get to know you," she insisted sadly. "They're worried that you're going to use my status for your own gain. They don't know...how we really feel."

"Well, maybe we should all sit down and talk or something," he suggested.

"Maybe," she mumbled. "But I want us to be mated first."

Danford nodded in response, unsure what to say, unsure what to do. He didn't want to be a doormat, but he also didn't want to take action and confront Freja's sisters; he just wanted things to work.

Freja then looked over her shoulder and frowned in confliction. "They're here," she said, glancing at Danford. "They're probably telling Greymore about us."

"What if we talk to them with Greymore?"

She sighed and looked down at her lap. It seemed as though she was thinking, and after a few moments, she glanced at him and said, "We can try."

"Right now?"

"Yeah."

He nodded and sat up. Although he was nervous, he felt like talking to them now was better than waiting. "Okay, let's go," he said, getting out of bed.

Freja followed him to the door.

Before he opened it, though, Danford said, "Wait," and pulled her closer. He kissed her lips and then gazed into her eyes for a moment, hoping that this wouldn't be the last time they were members of the pack, that this wasn't the last time Freja would see her sisters because of him.

She smiled at him and straightened his eyepatch. Then, she took his hand and began leading the way through the ship.

Danford's heart was racing—he was terrified. He'd never talked to Freja's sisters before, and he had no idea what they were like, but from what he'd seen and heard, they didn't seem very kind *at all*. But he'd do his best to put on a calm façade; the last thing he wanted was to give Freja's sisters another reason to berate him.

When they reached the lounge where they'd not long spoken to Greymore, Freja pulled the door open and stepped inside, pulling Danford with her. And there they were... Verity, Sophronia, and Opal, sitting around a table with Greymore at the head.

The very moment their eyes locked onto Danford, the three of them pulled looks of equal disgust. Verity jumped to her feet, and the other two followed suit.

"What the hell is that disgusting runt doing here?!" Verity shouted in revolt.

"Get out at once!" Sophronia yelled.

"Filthy rodent—let go of her!" Opal snapped, storming over.

Danford took the slightest step back, trying to grasp onto whatever confidence he could muster; he didn't want to look weak and embarrass Freja further.

The Luna gently shoved her sister back. "Back off, Opal," she warned, almost growling. "We've come here so that we can all have a civilized conversation about this." She pulled Danford closer, their sides meeting. "Whether the three of you like it or not, Danford is my fated mate, and I plan to seal the bond with him."

Her three sisters looked horrified.

"Freja, he's an Omega!" Sophronia exclaimed.

"Upsilon," Freja corrected. "And a very good runner. He's not some weak, useless little loser like you think he is. He's smart, he's kind, he's thoughtful, and above all of that, he makes me feel wanted. He makes me feel the kind of way I've dreamed of feeling since we were teenagers. You all found your mates, and I've spent *years* wondering if I'd ever find mine." She looked at Greymore. "And no offence, but I knew the second I saw him that Greymore wasn't my fated mate—"

"Same," Greymore muttered.

"—But I put up with it just like the three of you asked, and yet, here we are. It's *him*," she said, looking at Danford.

Danford's fear was accompanied by a hint of warmth, of relief. He loved that she was sticking up for him, and he wanted to say something, but he had no idea what he should say or if he should speak at all.

Verity crossed her arms and shook her head. "What would mother say? What would *Ada* say?"

Freja scoffed. "Do you think I give a rat's ass what Ada would think? She's dead! And we never followed her way anyway."

"She's still our line's ancestor," Opal argued. "Alphas marry Alphas, or at the very least, a Beta."

"But again, Ada. Is. Dead!" Freja shouted frustrated. "What? Do you think that she's going to come down from the sky and punish me? Ada isn't our Goddess, she's not our be-all and end-all. The Moon Goddess decides our fate. Mother would be shocked, sure, but she'd trust the Moon Goddess' decision, and so should you."

The three of them glanced at each other; while Verity and Opal's scowls thickened, Sophronia seemed to loosen up a little.

"Freja...I just..." Sophronia started. "We don't know him."

"So get to know him," Freja insisted. "Do you really think I'd put my life and my status on the line if he wasn't worth it?"

"You've always been reckless, Freja," Verity muttered.

The Luna scowled angrily at her sister. "Seriously, Verity? Were you not the one who hid your same-sex relationship from *everyone* for over a year? Scared that we wouldn't accept you or Imogen, scared that we'd cast you out. But *did* we? No. Because Imogen is your fated mate. *That* was all that mattered. Why can't you give me the same courtesy? The same trust?"

Sophronia then stepped forward and ushered Opal aside. She stood in front of Danford, looking him up and down. "What does my sister mean to you?" she questioned.

"Everything," he insisted. "Y-you have to understand that, even if she wasn't an Alpha, even if she wasn't a werewolf at all, I'd feel the same way about her. And I know that it's all happening very fast, and it's very new and we still have a lot to learn about each other, but I'd do anything for her, and there's nothing that I want in return…other than her love."

With a skeptical frown, Sophronia looked back at her sisters.

"So he says," Verity muttered.

"I mean it," Danford insisted.

Opal shook her head. "Do any of you have any idea how this is going to affect the pack?" she questioned and looked at Greymore. "Your marriage binds it together. What if they decide that this runt isn't good enough, huh? We'll split, we'll fight, and wolves will die!"

"The pack needs each other and they know it!" Freja interjected irritably. "Greymore and I are the Alphas; our word is law. If we tell them that Danford and I are mated, then that's that. If wolves want to leave, let them, but I know for a fact that they'll come crawling back."

"This isn't like you, Freja," Verity said, looking confused.

"Isn't it?" the Luna questioned. "You know barely anything about me, Verity."

"She's right," Sophronia said, turning to face Opal and Verity. She then sighed and shook her head in frustration. "This is all just…*a lot*. But…if Danford is our elder sister's true mate, we have no right to stop her from choosing to tie the bond."

"Are you joking?" Verity exclaimed. "He's a runt!"

"He's not good for you, Freja," Opal concurred.

"And you know that how? Rumours among the pack? Stories about when he was a rogue? Human parents? I know it all, Opal. He's told me everything that could possibly make me want to reject him, but I haven't. None of it matters to me. He could be the weakest Omega in the pack—he could be missing more than just an eye and I'd still be having this conversation with you. How many times do I have to say it?!"

Once more, the three of her sisters wordlessly glanced at one another.

"He's a good guy, man," Greymore mumbled. "Better than most I know."

Sophronia let out a deep, tired sigh, shifting her gaze to Greymore. "Do you think the pack will split?"

"I hope not," he replied.

"This is pure insanity," Verity exclaimed. "Are you *actually* considering letting this happen? Our own sister marrying a—"

"Just shut up, Verity," Sophronia snapped at her. "Or am I going to have to bring up the fact that we let you marry Imogen over Brent?"

Verity pouted and looked away like a stroppy child.

Sophronia then turned to Opal. "Surely you remember what it felt like before you found Roscoe?" she asked, frowning. "Do you really want to subject our sister to that kind of loneliness?"

Opal glanced at Danford, shifted her conflicted gaze to Freja, and then frowned at Sophronia. "No," she said with a sigh.

"Then it looks like it's settled," Sophronia said. "Two against one."

"This is just…just stupid!" Verity growled.

Ignoring her, Sophronia turned to face Danford and Freja. "Danford, Freja, you have my blessing. But—" she set a hostile glare on Danford, "—if I hear that you've used my sister in any way whatsoever, I won't hesitate to kill you. Understood?"

Danford shook his head, frowning almost. "I would never."

"You're actually believing this?" Verity called. "You've all lost your fucking minds."

Still ignoring her, Opal then stepped forward and stood beside Sophronia. "You have my blessing, too. But I'll be watching you very closely," she said to Danford, squinting at him.

He nodded, still fighting to keep his anxiety buried. "Thank you, both of you. I really appreciate it."

"I'll have nothing to do with this hypocrisy," Verity growled as she shoved past them all and left the room, slamming the door shut behind her.

Freja huffed irritably. "Why is she like this?"

"She's just grieving," Sophronia muttered. "Give her time."

Opal let out a deep sigh. "So, what now? Do we tear up the human marriage papers and have a big wedding or what?"

Greymore stood up and with a grunt. "We tell the pack, and we try to convince them to stay together under this new…situation," he answered.

"We should probably also tell Aleksei and Zalith," Freja said.

With a shake of his head, Greymore said, "Nah, not yet. They're up to their ears in Numen bullshit. We'll tell them when things cool off here. People are gonna be confused and stressed and maybe even angry for a while."

Danford wasn't ashamed to admit to himself that if Freja and Greymore had to stay together, he was happy being the man on the side who she loved more. He thought about suggesting it, but he was afraid of making Freja's sisters mad—he was afraid of upsetting Freja, too.

"Okay, we gotta work this out," Sophronia said. "Ideas? Anyone?"

No one said anything.

Danford clenched his jaw, conflicted. But he knew that Freja wanted the packs to stay together; he didn't want to curse her to a life alone out there. So he battled with the hesitation and said, "What if…well, what if Freja and Greymore stay married—I-I mean it *is* a business marriage after all, right? And…the pack know it. And then we just tell everyone that Freja's found her true mate; she and Greymore will remain marked, but…well…she and I can still be mated, right?"

"I mean…that might work," Sophronia said. "We'd have to make it very clear that you two are still the Alpha pair responsible for the pack, though."

"Only if Danny is completely comfortable with that," Freja said, looking at him. "During pack disputes, I'd have to talk and fight alongside Greymore as if he were my true mate."

He nodded stiffly. "That's fine…as long as you aren't making out and stuff.…"

Freja stifled a laugh. "There'll be nothing like that."

"Not interested—respectfully," Greymore chimed in.

Opal then said, "So…this is happening?"

Sophronia looked at Freja. "Sis?"

Freja exhaled deeply before smiling at Danford. "It is."

Danford smiled and nodded. He was happy—*so happy*—but he was nervous, too. Of course he was. This was a massive life change, but he was content knowing that his future would be with Freja.

"Everyone's a little drunk right now," Greymore said with a sigh. "I think we should get the whole ceremony thing done tomorrow afternoon once everyone's sobered up."

"Wait, so how does this work?" Opal asked.

Greymore leaned against the minibar and poured himself a shot of whisky. "Freja and I remain marked or claimed or whatever it's called, and she and Danny seal the fated bond. This definitely ain't the first time something like this has happened—and I mean…we all got two shoulders, right?" he muttered, sounding a little amused.

"Sounds complicated," Sophronia said with a sigh.

"Not really," Freja said. "You remember Nina's pack, right? That whore had seven claims *and* her fated bond."

Sophronia and Opal snickered.

"Who's Nina?" Danford mumbled.

"Some Alpha that Aleksei had to deal with a while back. She was trying to unite the packs and start a war. He killed her and all her little fuckboys," Freja said, smirking.

Greymore suddenly handed a shot to Danford.

"Oh, thanks," he said.

Once he returned to the bar, Greymore asked, "Ladies?"

"Sure," Opal replied.

"Not me," Sophronia said, placing her hand on her heavily pregnant belly.

"No, thanks," Freja replied.

As he sipped from his shot, Danford smiled a little. They were lucky that Greymore was pretty progressive and wasn't hung up on old traditions and laws.

"Well," Greymore said as he handed Opal her drink. "I'm happy it's you, Danny, and not one of those other dickheads out there," he chuckled.

Danford laughed a little, too. "Thank you for being so understanding, Greymore. I really didn't want to cause any trouble."

"You're fine, don't worry," Greymore assured him.

Freja then smiled at Danford. "Should we have the ceremony in the dell?"

"Who's going?" he asked.

"It'd be everyone, right?" Sophronia asked.

"Yeah," Greymore answered. "Whole pack's gotta witness it."

Danford fiddled with his shot glass. "I mean I'd like to do it at the dell, but I don't want people knowing about that spot."

"There's always the grove," Opal said. "That place is massive."

He looked at Freja.

"Yeah, sounds good," she said with a nod.

"All right, I'll make sure everyone's there tomorrow at noon," Greymore said.

Danford's anxiety suddenly intensified so much that he stifled a breath. The fact that he was pretty much getting married tomorrow hit him, and while he was excited and happy about it, he also asked himself if he was being stupid. He hoped not. But this was how these things went, wasn't it? Wolves found their fated mate and sealed the bond quickly. And he already knew that he loved Freja. He wanted to be with her for as long as she'd have him, and sealing their connection was the very sign he needed to know that their future together was solid…no matter what.

Chapter Sixteen

➺ ☽ �ू ☾ ⤚

Conflicts

| Monday, Primis 2nd, 960(TG)—Nefastus |

Rapid banging on the door woke Danford from his sleep. He frowned as he opened his eyes, but when he saw and felt Freja beside him, his confusion was overshadowed by relief and happiness. Every morning before, she'd been gone when he woke, but not this time, and it made his heart beat a little faster as the contentedness became overbearing.

But the knocking didn't stop. It only grew more insistent. And surprisingly, it didn't wake Freja—either that or it had but she didn't want to get up, which was fine. Danford would deal with whoever it was. A part of him worried, though, that it might be angry packmates. *Should* he answer? He listened…waiting, but he only heard one pair of footsteps and one faint heartbeat.

He got out of bed, pulled on some trousers, a shirt, and his eyepatch, and headed to the door. When he pulled it open, though, he was greeted by *Peris*, and she looked distraught.

"Danny!" she exclaimed, huffing and puffing.

"W-what?" he asked, worried that she was about to give him news that he *really* didn't want to hear.

"You're…you're mating with *her*?" she questioned, frowning confusedly.

Danford pulled the door shut behind him, hoping to spare Freja from whatever was about to happen. "Y-yeah, I am," he said with a nod.

Peris pouted sadly. "But she's an Alpha, and her sisters hate you."

"Well…it seems like only *one* of them hates me," he said, dragging his hand over the back of his head. He wasn't sure what he felt right now. Bad because it was so sudden and he hadn't had a chance to tell her himself? Confused because he'd never shown any romantic interest in Peris, so the jealousy in her eyes made no sense?

"B-but…but why?" she asked, getting a little teary-eyed.

"Because I love her, and she's my fated mate," he answered confidently.

She shook her head. "W-what if she rejects you? She still can, you know, and I think she will. You're just an Upsilon, Danny; you should be with someone of your own rank."

Danford was admittedly getting tired of being reminded that he was just an Upsilon and Freja was an Alpha. It didn't matter, did it? The Moon Goddess had made them fated to one another, and their bond was predestined. Freja had made it clear that she wanted to be with him no matter what, and he trusted her. "She's not going to reject me," he told Peris. "We're sealing the bond."

Peris' distraught expression thickened. "Why *wouldn't* she reject you? Th-the pack are gonna go wild about this—they could chase you out!"

"Because she doesn't care about ranks or old traditions," he said almost irritably— he was starting to get annoyed; why did he have to explain himself?

"*Everyone* cares about ranks and traditions; it's how werewolves work!"

"Peris, we already talked this through with Greymore; everything's going to be okay. You don't have to worry."

"But I *am* worried. How do you know she's not going to change her mind?"

"I just do, and I understand that life has its own twists and turns, but if we don't take risks at all, then what's the point?"

She pouted, glaring at him. It looked like she was going to say something, but she didn't; she turned around as she sniffled, and then she stormed off.

He started feeling guilty. "Peris," he called.

Peris stopped and glared over her shoulder at him.

"I don't know why you're upset, but I'm sorry. I promise it's all under control."

"You don't know why I'm upset?" she questioned angrily, turning to face him. She scoffed and said, "I thought we were friends—that…maybe we'd be more than that someday." With a despondent scowl, she looked away from him. "I guess I was wrong."

"Oh…" he responded, feeling awkward and even more guilty. He didn't really know what to say, either. "Sorry, Peris."

She huffed angrily, and then she turned around and walked off.

Danford watched her leave. He felt bad knowing that Peris thought they'd become more than friends, and he still didn't know what to say to her. But he had a lot more to worry about today; he'd work out what to tell her later.

With a quiet sigh, he headed back into his room.

"Everything okay?" Freja asked.

"I don't know," he mumbled as he sat down beside her. "I think so."

"What did she want?"

"Basically that she's into me and she's mad that you and I are together."

Freja rolled her eyes. "She's known you for like a day."

Danford laughed a little. "Well, *we've* known each other for four days."

Amused, she sat up and ran her fingers through his hair. "We're fated, so it's natural how fast things have happened for us."

He smiled at her, and then he said, "I hope she'll be okay."

"Maybe she'll find her fated mate at the ceremony," she suggested.

"Maybe," he said as he pondered. "I wonder if it's the wolf she was talking about still out there in the forest—Ray."

"Greymore's guys will probably find him eventually, so I suppose we'll see," she said, resting her head on his shoulder. "Are you nervous about today?"

"Very," he said with a light chuckle. "Are you?"

Freja nodded. "I remember my sister's ceremony; it was like a proper, huge wedding," she said, almost with a longing tone in her voice.

"Sorry we won't be able to do anything like that," Danford said sadly. "I'd give it to you if we had time."

She shrugged and said, "Maybe in a few years when things are calm enough for Greymore and me to unclaim each other; we could get human married if you like."

Danford smiled. "That would be very nice actually. Maybe we'll be able to get a house with a lot of land and we can make ourselves somewhere cosy so we can sleep outside," he said contently.

"That sounds nice. From what I've seen, there's a lot of space out near the compound, so we also wouldn't really have to be too far from the pack."

"Do you like to garden?" he asked her. "My mom had a huge vegetable garden in the backyard, and I always wanted to grow my own, but it's harder than she made it seem," he said with a quiet laugh. "Or maybe plants just hate me, I don't know."

"My grandma was the pack chef, so I know a thing or two about growing vegetables, but that's about it," she said with a fond smile.

"Oh, that's fair. I guess you were basically a princess."

"Ugh, don't remind me," she said with a playful huff. "Nobody wanted to let me do anything. My sisters and I took part in a lot of sneaking around when we were younger."

Danford was admittedly surprised by that because her sisters were so adamant about the rules recently that they felt the need to turn her in. "How did they take it when you became Alpha?" he asked curiously.

"Verity was mad. She thought she out-classed me at every turn, but that's just how she is. Sophronia was happy for me, and Opal didn't really say much. At the time, I was ecstatic…until I learned how much work it was. But as I got older, I kinda just got the hang of things. Verity's always been bitter and takes whatever chance she can get to undermine me, but I've learned to put up with it."

"Well, I hope she means well."

"Verity never means well. We're always going to have that eldest and second-eldest sister rivalry going on. But she'd never do anything to intentionally hurt me...at least I hope not," she said with a light chuckle.

Danford smiled, hiding a grimace; if he had siblings, he'd never be like that. "That sounds stressful."

"She gets it from our dad. He was the over-protective, in-love-with-the-rules type. But it was the rules he loved so much that got him killed in the end, so," she said with a shrug.

"Oh...." He didn't really know what to say to that.

"The vampires were offering a treaty, talking about calling a ceasefire. The deal was that we'd agree to live peacefully among the humans and vampires, but my dad was obsessed with the ancient law about, uh...it was said some poetic, old-Deiganish way, but the gist of it was that werewolves and vampires would remain enemies no matter what. My mom and grandma wanted to accept Aleksei's terms, but my dad? He decided to go behind their backs with the pack's strongest and launch a stealth attack on one of Aleksei's coven homes. My dad was the only one who made it out, but he died days later from all the vampire venom," she mumbled, sounding sad but irritated.

Danford frowned sullenly. "Oh, I'm sorry to hear that."

She shrugged, lifting her head to look over at the window. "He wasn't the greatest person, my dad...but I did love him." She scoffed and shook her head. "He didn't even acknowledge his mistake, either; he blamed everyone but himself. And even when Aleksei offered to spare his life when my mother accepted the deal in his place, he refused. Prideful asshole."

"Why *did* you start working for Aleksei?" he asked curiously. "From a werewolf's perspective—at least Aegisguardian ones—he doesn't seem like the kind of person you'd sit across a table from."

"I never shared my predecessor's beliefs; I never followed Ada's way, or the apparent advice of my dad. I've done things my own way, and for the better of the pack. Siding with Aleksei was the best thing for us since war was brewing between the packs after Ada failed to unite them. He's kept us safe, he's given us somewhere to live, money to buy whatever we need—I have no reason to hate him as much as my dad did."

"You're very brave for that, you know. A lot of people feel pressured to do things because of their families."

She nodded. "I suppose, but—"

A loud, frantic knock came at the door, snatching both their attention.

Danford tensed up a little. He waited for Freja to pull her shirt on, and then he headed to the door and pulled it open.

"Danny," Clara huffed, looking flustered. "You should probably get up on deck. Peris, the new Omega, she's hollering out a whole lot of stuff, riling everyone up."

His eyes widened a little. "What's she saying?"

"Something about you and Freja being together?" she said unsurely.

"We are," Freja said, pulling the door the rest of the way open as she stood beside Danford, fully clothed.

"Oh…I'm so sorry for disturbing you," Clara said. "I didn't know what to tell them, but…she's still going." She glanced up, and the distant shouting and clamouring echoed through the floors above. "I went to Greymore first, but I thought I'd come to you next and let you know."

He looked at Freja. "We should go," he said worriedly.

She nodded in agreement, and as Clara led the way, they headed through the ship and up onto the deck.

Almost *everyone* was shouting and arguing, and Peris was riling them up.

"They'll leave us to deal with the other hostile packs!" she called, standing in the middle of the crowd. "We mean nothing to them!"

"She's raving," a man muttered.

"I heard it from him myself!" Peris insisted. "I saw them sneaking off!"

"Says the Omega," a woman scoffed.

"She has a point," someone said. "I saw them go off together last night."

"And not just last night!" Peris called. "The night before that, too! Can't you see? Our Alphas are going to reject each other, and then we'll be forced to fight, and whoever's left will either have to join up to the winner's pack or die!"

Unsettled murmurs echoed through the crowd.

"There they are!" someone then yelled.

The moment they saw Danford and Freja on the deck, the crowd flooded over like a tsunami, their questions a rapid flurry of distorted voices.

"Shut up!" Freja yelled.

The crowd slowly quietened down, and they went near silent when Greymore stepped up onto the deck and stood beside the Luna.

"What's going on here?" Greymore demanded.

Everyone glanced at each other.

"Is it true that little Danny and our Luna are sneaking around?" Edward asked.

"There's no sneaking around—not anymore," Freja answered and took hold of Danford's hand, causing gasps of shock, disgusted mutters, and anxious murmurs to ooze from the staring pack. "We're fated, and we're going to seal our bond today."

"You can't!" Peris shouted. "Our Alpha and Luna have to remain—"

"Greymore and I will keep our claims," Freja interjected.

"We'll still be together for the sake of the pack and tradition," Greymore chimed in. "But you *all* knew that this day would come for us one day or another; Freja and I were never fated."

"He's not wrong," Clara said. "They married to join our packs together. So long as they stay claimed, they—"

"It's not right!" Solomon growled.

"There's nothing within the ancient laws and traditions that say this isn't allowed to happen," Freja said firmly. "There's no way that any of you haven't heard about Nina or some other Alpha who was part of a polyamorous relationship or was married to someone and fated to another. You're all just being dramatic."

Danford stood there, watching as some of his packmates eyed him as if he were the shit on their shoe, while others feared for their futures. The guilt was overbearing, and he wondered if he should say something, but Freja and Greymore seemed to have it under control.

"We're not splitting the pack or shifting leadership or anything like that *at all*," Greymore assured them. "Again, Freja and I will remain claimed, thus, the pack will remain intact. Danford and Freja are not claiming or marrying or anything pack-affecting like that, all they are doing is sealing their fated bond. Now does anyone not understand that and need me to repeat it—keeping in mind how much I hate repeating myself?"

The pack glanced and murmured for a few long, tense moments.

"So...we're not gonna fight?" someone asked.

Greymore sighed deeply.

"No one's fighting anyone," Freja grumbled irritably. "Nothing is changing."

"Nothing's changing?" Solomon exclaimed. "This isn't right!"

"Shut up, Sol," Eldora snapped. "You're just against anything Danny-related because you blame him for Rowena's death."

"Eldora!" Clara snapped, slapping her arm.

"Someone had to say it!"

Being reminded about Rowena made the guilt constricting Danford worse; he still wished he could have done more, but there really wasn't anything he could have done to prevent her death.

"Alphas marry Alphas!" Peris insisted.

"Alphas marry Alphas!" someone deep within the crowd repeated.

And several others chanted the same thing...over, and over and over—

"Enough!" Greymore bellowed. "You're all being fucking ridiculous; one of the strongest, unchanging laws of our kind is that an Alpha's word is law, right? So listen the fuck up: Danny and Freja are sealing their bond at noon, and *all* of us are going to attend. Freja and I will remain marked, and the pack will stay together, strong as ever. *That* is law."

The pack murmured again.

"He's right," Randy muttered.

One by one, the pack started slowly agreeing.

But Peris' distraught glare only grew thicker. "You can't all be serious?!"

"Peris, stop," one of the wolves from her old pack mumbled to her.

"No!" she snapped, shoving them aside.

"Peris…" Danford said worriedly, stepping forward. "Please, just calm down."

She scoffed at him, a scoff that made it clear that she didn't trust him anymore, a scoff that might very well be the confirmation of the ending of their friendship.

Danford's heart hurt a little; he didn't want to lose his friend despite having not known her very long, but he wasn't going to do this in front of everyone. He'd try and talk to Peris privately later.

"Are we going to have a problem?" Greymore then asked Peris.

Peris looked up at him, pouted, and set her glare back on Danford. "No, sir," she said and stepped back into the crowd.

Greymore then looked around at everyone. "Ceremony's at noon, as said." He looked up at the sun. "That gives you all three hours to get ready. Go cut your hair or shave or whatever. Look your best. I want everyone waiting up on deck in two and a half hours ready to head to the grove. Got it?"

The pack, although some were reluctant, called their words of confirmation.

"I'll find you two a little earlier than that," Greymore said to Freja and Danford.

They both nodded and then watched him head below deck.

Danford shifted his sights to the pack, watching as they slowly dispersed. He caught judgemental glares and disgusting glowers, jealous frowns and aggravated stares. But when he spotted the few people who shot him smiles and looked happy for him and Freja, he focused on the relief that made him feel—and the sheer happiness of being only hours away from sealing the fated bond with his mate.

Of course, he was still nervous as hell. His whole life was about to change. But he was ready. Knowing that he'd spend the rest of his days with Freja was all he needed to fight the anxiety. She was everything he'd ever wished for.

Chapter Seventeen

»—) 𝔢 (—«

Understanding

Infatuation consumed Danford like a slow-burning flame, warm and persistent, leaving him helpless to its pull. All he could do was sit at his desk, charcoal pencil in hand, pretending to work, though his eyes rarely left Freja. She stood gracefully in front of the wall mirror by the door, brushing her golden hair with long, steady strokes. The soft glow of the morning light caught the strands, making her hair gleam like spun gold, shimmering with every movement. His heart pounded as he watched her, entranced by the effortless beauty she carried in even the simplest of actions.

He had been trying to finish his drawing of her, the one he'd been working on since he bought that frame, but it felt impossible. Every time Freja was near, she became an unavoidable distraction—one that he couldn't and didn't want to resist. His gaze drifted to her reflection in the mirror, taking in the curve of her neck, the delicate movements of her fingers through her hair, the subtle rise and fall of her chest as she breathed. Each detail of her presence captured his senses, leaving him captivated and restless all at once.

His fingers hovered over the page, itching to capture her essence in his drawing, but it was as though no lines or shading could ever truly do her justice. Every time he tried, it fell short. He couldn't capture the way her golden locks glowed in the light, or the way her eyes—those fierce yet gentle eyes—held a power that both soothed and stirred him.

Danford sighed quietly, his gaze flickering between the half-finished sketch and Freja's reflection. It was maddening how completely she occupied his thoughts, how every inch of him seemed drawn to her like the moon to the tide. He knew he should focus, he knew that finishing this drawing was important, but how could he when the very subject of his work stood only a few feet away, making his heart race with every small movement?

As Freja tilted her head slightly, pulling her hair over one shoulder, Danford's breath hitched. He leaned forward, pencil poised, trying once more to capture the moment on paper. But the lines blurred, his focus faltering as a soft smile touched her lips. That smile—calm, confident, completely unaware of the chaos it stirred within him—rendered him powerless. How could a mere smile unravel him so completely?

He swallowed, his chest tightening with a mixture of admiration and longing. Infatuation didn't even begin to describe what he felt. Freja was more than just a distraction; she was his muse, his obsession, and the one thing he couldn't take his eyes off no matter how hard he tried.

And in the quiet moments like this, when it was just the two of them, the world outside ceased to matter. It was only her, and the way she effortlessly captivated every part of him.

"I can see you staring in the mirror, you know," she said with a smirk.

Flustered, Danford set his eyes back on his drawing. "Sorry."

She giggled, still brushing her hair. "Why are you sorry? I'm your mate; you can stare at me all you want."

He slowly set his eyes back on her and smiled, but then he glanced down at his drawing. Despite his happiness, he couldn't stop thinking about how upset Peris had been. Sure, she annoyed him a little earlier, but that didn't stop him from wanting to see if their friendship was saveable. They still had some time before they'd have to meet with Greymore, so while Freja got ready, he thought he could talk to Peris. Only if the Luna was comfortable with that, though.

Once he finished the shading he'd been working on, he gently pulled the fabric cover over his paper to both hide it from Freja and protect it from anything that might ruin it before he could frame it. "Uh…Freja," he said, looking across the room at her.

"Yes?" she drawled curiously.

"If it's okay with you, I wanna see if I can save my and Peris' friendship. She was really upset earlier, and—"

"She's crazy is what she is," the Luna muttered, curling her eyelashes. "Spreading all those lies, upsetting people. She's trouble."

Danford sighed deeply. "I think that she was only doing it because she was confused and upset. Aegisguardian werewolves do things differently, right? She probably believes that what she was saying is true because, in this world's case, it would be, right?"

Freja glanced at him. "I suppose."

"I'm not going to insist or anything, though. She kinda annoyed me earlier this morning, and if she's just going to try and convince me that we can't be mated, then I'll leave," he said, standing up.

The Luna put her lash curler down and turned to face him; she grabbed his arm when he was close enough and pulled him nearer. "And when you get back, there might be time for us to consummate before the ceremony," she flirted, her eyes searching his face as if it were a meal on a plate.

Danford was certain that his cheeks went a little red, but he did his best to hide his fluster. "That sounds good," he said, and then he looked at Freja's neck. "It looks really good on you," he said, brushing his fingertips over the constellation locket.

She smiled and lifted her arm to gaze at it. "I love it so much, and it's the perfect size for my wolf wrist, too, so I don't have to worry about taking it off."

"That's good," he said, and then he kissed her lips. "I'll try not to be too long."

She nodded, lowering her arm. "See you soon—oh, and if she gets any crazier than she was up on deck earlier, you should probably run."

He laughed nervously. "Y-yeah, I'll keep that in mind."

Danford left his room and navigated his way through the ship, finding his way to Jenna and Lila's room. He knocked, and when Lila answered, she looked him up and down with the same derogatory glare he'd gotten from his packmates earlier.

"Can I speak to Peris, please?" he asked.

Lila looked over her shoulder. "Peris, it's Danford."

"I don't wanna talk to him," came Peris' muffled, despondent voice.

"She doesn't want to talk to you," Lila relayed.

Danford sighed quietly. "Please, Peris," he called into the room. "Just hear me out."

"She said she—"

"It's fine," Peris muttered, pulling the door the rest of the way open.

Lila scoffed at Danford before walking off to join Jenna by the vanity.

Peris stared expectantly at him.

He glanced over her shoulder, seeing Lila and Jenna staring, clearly listening.

"Can we go somewhere private?" he asked her. "Like one of the lounges?"

With a deep sigh, she looked back at her roommates. "I'll be back soon."

"Call us if you need us," Jenna said.

Peris stepped out of the room and pulled the door shut behind her. Then, as he led the way, she followed Danford to the end of the hall and into the empty drinking lounge. He sat at one of the tables, and Peris sat across from him, tapping her fingers on the wooden surface while glaring expectantly at him.

Danford felt like *she* should be the one apologizing, but he understood that the wolves of Aegisguard had different rules and beliefs, so he wasn't going to make her feel like shit because of that. All he wanted to do was repair their friendship. "Look, I know that things are different for the werewolves here; you guys have your beliefs, and those of us from Eltaria have ours. I know that…it's tricky when the two packs come together over the kind of conflict or situation that happened earlier, but since the packs joined, we've all done our best to understand and respect each other, and—"

"Our laws and beliefs can't just change, Danny," she said with a pout. "We've all been raised this way."

"I know that, but *we 've* all been raised our way, too. Like I said, it's hard, but we try, and I'm asking *you* to try because you're my friend, and I *do* care about you."

"If you cared about me, why not tell me right away that something was going on between you and Luna Freja?"

"Because I didn't want to expose or embarrass Freja. You said it yourself, she's an Alpha and I'm an Upsilon. It's not common, but it's not impossible or completely unheard of—the fated bond *or* the situation with her and Greymore."

She shook her head.

Danford wasn't sure what was going on inside her head, whether she was trying to understand or not, but as much as it saddened him, he wanted to make sure that Peris understood all her options. "But this isn't the kind of place where you'll be forced to align yourself with our beliefs. Some wolves merely just respect the pack's mutual beliefs and laws and keep it out of pack politics. Others chose to leave."

"Leave? You mean go back out there as a rogue?" she questioned, astounded.

"You don't *have* to leave, Peris. You can just keep your beliefs out of pack politics and respect—"

"Yeah, respect the mutual beliefs, which were decided *how*, may I ask?"

"When Freja and Greymore got married, the pack voiced their previous pack or family traditions and such, and Greymore and Freja put everything together, and over the week, the entire pack came to agree on one set of rules and traditions," he explained. "You'd have been told this by now, but with the new year and the celebration, there hasn't been time."

Peris crossed her arms. "What are the laws and traditions?"

He exhaled deeply, taking a moment to recall everything. "Well, we don't have any rank restrictions when it comes to relationships; sure, everyone has their own private opinion, but we all collectively agreed that anyone can see anyone."

"So why sneak around with Freja?"

"Because she's married to Greymore, and if I'm being honest, I thought it was just a one or two-time thing."

She pouted and looked away.

Danford continued, "Like Greymore said, Alpha's word is law. If he says something, we do it."

"Yeah, I got that one."

"New pack members have to be with a supervising wolf whenever leaving the ship or camp," he said, recalling. "Uh…no starting conflicts with the people of the Citadel. Zalith and Aleksei's word is also law; we work for them, so when they give us a job, we do it."

Peris set her eyes back on him. "The demons, right?"

He nodded.

"When do I meet them?"

"Uh...well, it isn't likely that you'll see much of them. But I heard that they're coming to the little celebration that Greymore has planned for when the compound is ready, so you'll see them and some of the other demons then."

"I heard that you had a thing with the Zalith one," she said, looking intrigued, but she was clearly trying to hide any other emotion besides anger behind a frown.

Danford felt embarrassed and looked away from her for a moment. "It wasn't really a thing; we just had sex a few times."

"Does Freja know?"

"Of course she does," he said with a frown, turning his head to look at her.

"Hmm. Okay, what about traditions? Other than the one from yesterday."

"Well, at the beginning of winter, all the allied packs meet in a mutually agreed place and exchange pack members—"

"Yeah, the Winter Unity Oath," Peris interjected. "Jenna told me; it was how she and Lila met or something."

Danford nodded. "There's um...the Herald."

"Yeah, we have that here, too."

"Uh...oh, another rule is that nobody turns a human into a werewolf without the Alphas' permission," he said, remembering.

"I wouldn't wish being bitten on anyone, anyway," she muttered.

He tried to remember more rules and traditions, but he couldn't care less about them right now. "Peris...I still want to be your friend," he insisted. "I know that this whole Freja thing came as a shock, and I'm really sorry that I didn't tell you sooner—if I could have without making things difficult for her, I would have."

Peris sighed deeply and looked away. "It *was* a shock, and it still is."

"I know. To be honest, even I'm still reeling."

"I just..." she paused and huffed, setting her eyes on him. "I thought that maybe it was gonna be you."

"What was gonna be me?"

She flailed her arms frustratedly. "That you'd be my mate!" she exclaimed, starting to sound upset. "You helped me in that battle, you guided me and even took me to the city. I guess I just read it all wrong."

He frowned guiltily; he never meant to lead her on like that. "I really am sorry, Peris. I-I didn't realize that...I didn't know that was how you felt. I kinda suck at picking these things up, so I guess it's my fault, but—"

"No," she mumbled, shaking her head and losing her frustrated glare. "It's *my* fault. I always get attached too fast, and when...when I feel like I'm losing someone, I kinda just...freak out. Ever since I lost Ray, I haven't really been the same."

Danford understood. She'd lost her friend, the only wolf she'd been able to trust in that awful ex-pack of hers. Under Orson's cruel rule, he wasn't surprised that Peris and her packmates would come out of it traumatized and scarred. "I told Greymore about Ray," he said, hoping it might make her feel better. "If he's out there, we'll find him."

A weak smile broke through Peris' frown. "I don't know. A part of me's been wondering if I'm being too naïve. He's been out there for a long time; there are over a hundred things that could have happened to him."

He shook his head. "No, don't think like that. From what you've told me, he sounds like a fighter."

"Maybe," she mumbled. But then she sighed and leaned back in her seat. "Just promise me that you're not gonna be the kinda guy who gets hitched and then forgets about all of his friends. I do really like you, Danny, even if all we can be is friends. I don't wanna lose the only friend I've made here—well…I guess Lila and Jenna are my friends now, but…they're girls, and they talk about girl stuff, you know? I don't wanna talk about hair pomade and the new stylist on Florence Street; I wanna talk about hunting and tracking and which pack is invading which territory. I'm a wolf who turns into a human, not a human who turns into a wolf."

Everything she said made sense. "I understand," he said with a nod. "And don't worry. I'm not going to shove my friends aside or anything; I'll still have time to like…hang out or whatever." Unless Freja wasn't comfortable with that, but he wasn't going to say it. "Just…please try to accept the pack laws and traditions and refrain from using your own beliefs in pack politics."

Peris exhaled deeply and nodded. "Okay, I'll try." She then adorned a cautious expression and leaned closer. "I think I should warn you about Solomon," she said quietly. "He seems to really hate you; he blames you for his mate's death. I was just a listener at the time, but he was talking about stepping forward at the ceremony and trying to stop it."

Danford tensed up. The last thing he wanted was a fight breaking out at his and Freja's ceremony. He wasn't going to let anything ruin it. "All right, thanks for telling me, Peris."

She leaned back in her seat again. "I'm sorry for riling them all up earlier. I was just…overwhelmed—and I know that's no excuse, but it was a lot for me to process; so much has been happening lately."

"Yeah, I know. It's a lot to try and get used to. New wolves, new territory, new traditions, laws, etcetera. Anyone would be overwhelmed. And I accept your apology, but I think you should say sorry to Greymore and Freja, too."

Peris didn't look uncomfortable or irritated by his suggestion. "Yeah, you're right."

"Later, though—maybe after the ceremony."

She nodded, and then she exhaled and smiled. "So...will you be Danny Greymore or Danny Ardelean? Or Danny whatever-your-last-name-is."

He laughed nervously. "Well, to be honest, I think I'd take Freja's name—she's the Alpha, after all."

"Hmm...Danford Ardelean. It has a nice ring to it," she said with a giggle.

"It does," he agreed, his smile growing. But he couldn't sink into the content of relief just yet; he had to tell Greymore about Solomon. "Thank you for hearing me out," he said appreciatively. "Like we said, I know there's been a lot going on, but I wanted to make sure you're okay."

"Me, too," she said with a smile. "And thank you for coming to me. To be honest, I was afraid that I'd screwed things up and that there was no point in trying to explain myself. When you came to my room, I thought you were coming to tell me that you hated me or something."

Danford shook his head. "I mean I was a little annoyed, sure, but I wouldn't hate you."

"Sorry I annoyed you."

"It's fine. It's in the past."

"Do you think that...well, should I try to calm Solomon down?" she suggested.

"No, it's okay. He can be kinda...unpredictable. I'll just tell Greymore, and he'll deal with the situation."

She nodded and said, "Okay. If I can help, let me know."

"Yeah, I will," he said as he stood up. "I'll let you get back to getting ready, but I'll see you at the ceremony, yeah?"

Peris got up, too. "Yeah. And...congrats, Danny," she said and hugged him for a few moments.

"Thank you," he said, reciprocating her hug.

Then, Peris stepped back and smiled at him. "See you later."

He nodded and watched her leave the room. That went better than he thought it might, and to his relief, Peris and he were still friends. He just hoped that Freja was comfortable with it and there wouldn't be any problems later down the line. He wasn't going to stand there and overthink, though. He had to get to Greymore.

Danford left the lounge and made his way through the ship to Greymore's room. He knocked, and when his boss called him in, he opened the door and set his eyes on his Alpha, who was sprawled out on his couch with a plate of cheese and meat.

When Greymore saw him, he groaned a little. "Please don't tell me someone else is starting a war or some shit up on deck."

"N-no, I just...well I talked with Peris, and we fixed things, but she told me that Solomon is planning on stepping forward at the ceremony and trying to stop it."

Greymore rolled his eyes. "Fucking Solomon," he murmured with his mouth full. "I'll deal with him, don't worry. Anyone else I should be aware of?"

"Peris didn't mention anyone else, but…well, I'd imagine that Solomon's friends might be in on it, too," he suggested.

"Right, yeah," Greymore muttered and then waved his hand dismissively while stuffing more cheese into his mouth. "Go…be with Freja. I'll come get you later."

With a nod, Danford left his room and walked through the ship once more. The halls were buzzing with a mixture of excited and conflicted chatter, but he wasn't going to let anything drag him from the happiness he'd found himself ensnared in. No, nothing could take away the sheer joy that *devoured* him, that pulsed through his veins. A life he never thought he'd have was just an hour away, and he was ready for it—*more than* ready. He just had to try his best to be patient for the next sixty minutes.

Chapter Eighteen

>—) 𝕮 (—«

The Bond

D anford walked beside Freja, following Greymore with the pack in tow. They headed to the tree line, and once they passed it, everyone shifted into their wolf forms. The further into the forest they got, the faster Danford's heart raced. He was so nervous that he felt like he might throw up, but he did his best to keep a hold of himself.

It was happening. They were on their way to the grove, and it wasn't very far away now. His legs were shaking, and his body felt tense; his mind was racing, a thousand thoughts spinning around inside his head, but the one that screamed the loudest at him was: what if Freja regretted it? What if she decided that she didn't want to spend the rest of her life with him? There was a part of him that was terrified she'd reject him, but… wouldn't she have done so by now? Why wait until the ceremony?

He glanced at her, but the moment he saw her beautiful face, his worries began withering. How could he think so negatively of her? No, he trusted her. He'd made the decision to trust her days ago, and he didn't regret it, nor would he let his anxious thoughts rule him. This was the happiest day of his life; he was about to walk into a future with his mate, whom he never thought he'd find. There was nothing that could take his contentment away.

The pack continued their trek through the forest, the lively chatter of the wolves creating a soft hum in the air. Danford listened as snippets of conversation reached his ears, and it surprised him to hear more positive talk than there had been earlier. It seemed that some of the wolves who had been against his union with Freja were now speaking with a lighter tone, their doubts slowly giving way to acceptance. Maybe, just maybe they were beginning to see the bond he shared with her in a different light. His heart swelled with quiet relief.

As they walked, the trees began to thin out, giving way to a clearing, and the chatter only grew more excited. They had reached the grove.

Danford's breath caught as he stepped into the grove. It was as if they had crossed a threshold into a hidden world, one untouched by time. The tall trees that surrounded the space stood like ancient guardians, their trunks thick and gnarled, their branches twisting overhead to form a natural canopy. Golden sunlight streamed through gaps in the leaves, casting shimmering beams of light onto the forest floor like a scattering of stars. The air was cool, fresh with the faintest hint of pine and damp earth, mingling with the soft scent of wildflowers that blanketed the ground in small clusters of white, purple, and yellow. It was a peaceful, almost sacred place, a sanctuary tucked away in the heart of the forest.

The grove was shaped by nature's careful hand—a circle of old oaks and elms, their leaves still clinging despite the cool bite of winter. Moss-covered rocks lined the perimeter, as though placed intentionally, forming a natural boundary between the forest beyond and the sanctity of the grove within. Near the centre, a small river wound its way through the clearing, its clear waters babbling softly over smooth stones. The sound of the flowing water was soothing, a gentle backdrop to the rising excitement of the pack.

Each Beta broke formation and began instructing where the wolves would stand or sit, positioning them in a wide circle around the centre of the grove. Greymore led Danford and Freja toward the small river, their steps quiet as they moved through the soft grass. Danford's heart raced with anticipation, his chest tightening with a mixture of nerves and excitement. This was it—the place Freja had told him about, the spot where their bond would be sealed.

They reached the riverbank, where the sunlight filtered through the trees in perfect alignment. It was just as Freja had described—a place of serenity and beauty, a place where the sunlight seeped through the leaves in golden streams, illuminating the water and the grass around it. The beams of light seemed almost alive, dancing gently across the surface of the river, creating an ethereal glow that bathed the entire area in warmth. Danford could see why it was so desired as a resting place—the sun's rays here seemed to offer not only warmth but peace, as if the very ground held a quiet promise of safety.

Now, though, it wasn't simply a place of rest. This place, with its golden light and soft river sounds, would now serve as the sacred spot where he and Freja would seal their bond. Danford stood still for a moment, taking in the beauty of it all—the sunlight glinting off the water, the way the trees seemed to lean in, almost as if they were witnesses to this moment. Freja stood beside him, her presence warm and reassuring, and he couldn't help but glance at her, feeling the weight of the moment settle around them.

This was where their union would become something more than just a bond forged in the fires of shared struggle and desire. Here, in this grove, under the watchful eyes of their pack and the ancient trees, they would become truly inseparable—bound not just by fate but by choice.

Danford exhaled softly, his heart steadying as he prepared for what was to come. The grove, with all its beauty and serenity, would forever be etched into his memory, the place where he and Freja would take the final step towards their forever. And as nervous as he was, he longed for the moment their new lives began.

Freja smiled at him as they stood facing each other, their sides to the pack. "Are you ready?" she asked excitedly.

He nodded shyly. "Are you?"

She nodded, too.

As he left them by the river to join the crowd, Greymore said, "It's down to you guys now."

Danford's heart raced faster, thumping as if it was going to burst from his chest. He had no idea whether he was supposed to say or do anything, but all his nervousness would let him do was stare at Freja wide-eyed.

Freja, on the other hand, seemed to know exactly what to do—of course she did. She was raised a wolf, far more familiar with these traditions than he was. Danford had always felt a bit out of place in situations like this, but now, standing before her, he felt that unfamiliar nervousness creep up again. Freja stepped forward, her golden eyes steady and reassuring as she nuzzled the side of his muzzle, sending a soft shiver down his spine.

She leaned into his ear, her voice a warm whisper against his fur, "You gently bite between my neck and left shoulder first; not too deep, but deep enough to leave a wound—it'll heal, don't worry. Then, I'll do the same to you, okay?"

He nodded, though his smile trembled with nerves. This was the moment that would bind them, that would change everything, and the weight of that responsibility pressed down on him. As Freja stepped back and stared at him expectantly, a flicker of hesitation gripped him. He didn't want to hurt her, even though she assured him it would heal. But this was necessary, an essential part of their bond.

With a deep breath, he fought through his reluctance and moved closer. Freja's gaze never wavered, her golden fur shimmering in the soft beams of light filtering through the trees, grounding him with her calm. Slowly, he widened his jaws and edged his muzzle toward her neck, his heart racing as he closed the distance. The warmth of her body and the trust in her stance calmed him just enough; when the space between her neck and shoulder was within his grasp, he gently bit down, careful to hold back the full strength of his jaws.

The moment his teeth pierced her skin, he braced himself for a flinch or a grunt, but Freja didn't move. In fact, she stood there almost serenely, her body relaxed, her breath steady, as though the bite was no more than a simple touch. A quiet, almost purring sound escaped her, and Danford's nerves began to fade. Her trust, her willingness to let him mark her in this way… it meant everything.

As soon as the faint taste of her blood reached his tongue, he pulled back, his heart pounding in his chest. The mark was there, his mark, now etched into her body—a symbol of their connection, of their union. He stepped back, his legs trembling slightly with the weight of it all, anticipation and excitement filling him.

Freja turned her head, golden eyes locking onto his with a quiet intensity. She smiled—a soft, knowing smile that reassured him once more—and then she stepped forward. His breath hitched as she closed the distance, nuzzling his neck as he had hers. She didn't need to ask him if he was ready. He already knew what was coming next.

Danford stood still, heart pounding as Freja opened her jaws and lowered her muzzle to the space between his neck and shoulder. Her warm breath washed over his fur, sending a shiver down his spine. Then, with a gentleness that surprised him, she bit down, her sharp teeth breaking the skin, leaving her own mark on him.

It wasn't the pain that filled his mind—it was the significance of it all, the overwhelming sense of belonging. The bite was deeper than just skin; it was a bond, a claim, a promise. Freja's touch made him feel whole, as if all the empty spaces in his heart were suddenly filled. He could feel her strength in the bite, but more than that, he could feel her love, her acceptance of him.

When she pulled back, her mark freshly imprinted on his skin, Danford exhaled deeply, his entire body trembling. Freja looked into his eyes, her gaze soft yet powerful, and in that moment, everything around them seemed to fall away. The pack, the forest, the traditions—none of it mattered. It was just the two of them, standing together in this grove, bound forever by something far greater than either of them could have imagined.

He couldn't hold back the smile that spread across his face, relief and joy washing over him in equal measure. Freja moved closer again, brushing her muzzle against his in a quiet, affectionate gesture. Her warmth surrounded him, soothing the lingering nerves and replacing them with a deep sense of peace.

"You're mine now," she whispered softly, her voice carrying the weight of the promise they had just made to each other.

Danford nodded, his throat tight with emotion. "And you're mine."

Freja pressed her body against his, and for a moment, they simply stood there, bathed in the soft glow of the grove. The sunlight filtered through the trees, casting golden patterns across their fur, and Danford knew that this moment—this place—would forever be etched in his memory. The grove, once just a quiet sanctuary, was now the birthplace of their bond, the place where they had sealed their fate.

He pulled back slightly, his eyes searching hers. "I love you," he murmured, his voice low, almost breathless. Saying it out loud felt strange, but it also felt like a huge weight off his shoulders. He *did* love her, and he couldn't wait to see where they'd go from this moment on.

Freja smiled again, a soft, beautiful smile that lit up her entire face. "I love you, too." Her response was a massive relief, one with no words to explain.

And then the pack howled, calling their congratulations.

Danford's smile widened, almost becoming a grin as uncontainable joy lit up his face. His heart raced, pounding in his chest in sync with the happiness swelling within him. Each beat seemed to pulse with pure, unfiltered emotion, warmth spreading through his entire body like a rising tide. A shiver ran down his spine—not from the cold, but from the sheer intensity of the moment. The overwhelming surge of happiness coursed through his veins like fire, igniting every nerve. His muscles tingled with excitement, and his skin prickled with the sensation of being truly, fully alive. In this perfect, fleeting moment, he trembled—not with nervousness or fear, but with the profound realization that this was real. Freja was his, and he was hers, bound together in a way that nothing could ever break.

Whatever the future held, Danford knew he was ready to face it—with Freja by his side, there was nothing they couldn't conquer.

FORBIDDEN BOND
A Numenverse Companion Story

THE NUMEN CHRONICLES
SERIES ONE

Nosferatu
The Numen Chronicles | Volume 1

✝

Demon's Fate
The Numen Chronicles | Volume 2

✝

Light
The Numen Chronicles | Volume 3

✝

Demon's Bane
The Numen Chronicles | Volume 4

✝

Ascendant
The Numen Chronicles | Volume 5

✝

Icarus
The Numen Chronicles | Volume 6

✝

Demon's Curse
The Numen Chronicles | Volume 7

✝

Renascence
The Numen Chronicles | Volume 8

✝

Demon's Reclamation
The Numen Chronicles | Volume 9

✝

[And more…]

THE NUMENVERSE
OTHER SERIES/STORIES

Aldergrove Chronicles

Set in the year 1176 after Aegisguard's second world war. After being told he has only six months left to live, Clementine decides to track down his sister's murderers, leading him to Aldergrove Academy, a place where a hundred students must fight to the death to earn their right to travel to the New World. But he soon learns that the students aren't the only ones prowling the corridors at night in search of blood.

✝

Where The Wild Wolves Have Gone

Set in the year 1330. Following Luan, a young transman werewolf who belongs to a pack owned by Lyca Corp., a military-focused organization. The pack have served them for generations, but after a mission goes sideways, Luan begins to learn the horrifying truth about the people they serve.

✝

Greykin Chronicles

Set in the year 1332, following Jackson, a journalist who heads to the snowy mountains of Ascela in search of his missing best friend, Wilson. But he discovers that not only is there a whole different world hidden out there, but death isn't necessarily the end for some creatures.

✝

The Numen Chronicles Series Two

Set in the year 1335. While hunting for his missing friend, Elijah stumbles upon a fiery journalist, who so happens to be looking for the same people as him: the doctors who experimented on him when he was a child. But when the two are forced to go on the run together, Elijah's healing wounds are opened, and he realises that Lyca Corp. took more than his childhood.

To stay up to date with future releases, follow the author through their website!

www.numenverse.com/

FORBIDDEN BOND
A Numenverse Companion Story

FORBIDDEN BOND
A Numenverse Companion Story

Milton Keynes UK
Ingram Content Group UK Ltd.
UKHW040439031224
452051UK00005B/29

9 781917 270021